"Surprise, surprise! I've come back to you, Lucinda."

Leo's eyes were blazing, but he sounded as smooth as any lover. "Well," he said finally, "what have you got to say for yourself?"

Lucinda found her voice, "I can explain," she promised.

"I'll bet you can." His chin jutted uncompromisingly. "I seem to remember you work in a library. I didn't realize you created the fiction for it, too."

"I know it looks that way—" She twisted her fingers. "When people, when my family finds out the truth, they're *really* going to have something to talk about."

"I think there's a way you might come out unscathed." She stared at him uncomprehendingly as he went on. "We could act out the lie. Pretend to be in love."

"Why?" she demanded. "Why would *you* go along with such a crazy scheme?"

"Oh, I want something in return, of course...."

Celia Scott, originally from England, came to Canada for a vacation and began an ''instant love affair'' with the country. She started out in acting but liked romance fiction and was encouraged to make writing it her career when her husband gave her a typewriter as a wedding present. She now finds writing infinitely more creative than acting since she gets to act out all her characters' roles, and direct, too.

Books by Celia Scott

Don't miss any of our special offers. Write to us at the following address for information on our newest releases.

Harlequin Reader Service
901 Fuhrmann Blvd., P.O. Box 1397, Buffalo, NY 14240
Canadian address: P.O. Box 603,
Fort Erie, Ont. L2A 5X3

Rumor
Has It

Celia Scott

Harlequin Books

TORONTO • NEW YORK • LONDON
AMSTERDAM • PARIS • SYDNEY • HAMBURG
STOCKHOLM • ATHENS • TOKYO • MILAN

ISBN 0-373-03040-1

Harlequin Romance first edition March 1990

For Jacqui

CHAPTER ONE

LUCINDA HAD JUST SETTLED down with her well-worn copy of *The Adventures of Huckleberry Finn* when the door of the upstairs sitting room flew open and her stepmother burst in. "Why Cindy! What are you doing indoors?" she exclaimed, then, catching sight of the book in Lucinda's hand she added, "I should think you get enough of books working in that stuffy old library all year."

"It's not stuffy," said Lucinda patiently. Ever since she'd started working at the library her family made this kind of comment at least once a day. "And anyway, you know I like reading."

"You don't say!" Fran Wainwright gave a little laugh, and Lucinda steeled herself, because that usually meant Fran, who was about as sensitive as a charging rhino, was about to say something thoughtless. "I declare, it's a miracle you don't have to wear thicker glasses than you do," she said now, going to the little desk that had belonged to Lucinda's mother. She started searching through the pigeonholes. "You haven't seen my checkbook around, have you, honey?"

Lucinda shook her head, and her fine, shoulder-length hair began slipping out of its ribbon. Since it was as silky as a baby's, it always seemed to be drooping out of the ribbons and barrettes she used in a futile attempt to keep it tidy. A pale brown strand fell across her eyes, and she hooked it behind her delicately modeled ear.

Fran pushed a pile of papers to one side. "I could have sworn I left my checkbook in here. I was here when I made out the check to the tennis club. I know I was. Em's probably been clearing up. I do wish she'd learn to leave things be."

"She hasn't been near this room," said Lucinda, coming quickly to the old housekeeper's defense. "I'm sure it'll turn up soon enough."

"Not soon enough to give her the housekeeping check." Fran straightened her back and tucked her checked shirt into the waistband of her slacks—a waistband that was remarkably small for a woman of forty-six. She was tall and had a fashionably boyish figure. Friends often said they had difficulty distinguishing her from her two daughters. They didn't have difficulty distinguishing her from her stepdaughter, however, since Lucinda was only five foot three and all rounded curves. "The fat one of the family," Fran always said.

"Well, Em will just have to wait for her old housekeeping, that's all." She went to the window and stared down at the sea, which was only just visible through a mist of rain. "I sure hope this weather improves. It'll be such a disappointment to your daddy if it louses up his sailing."

"Dad never lets a little thing like weather stop him," remarked Lucinda, shuddering at the memory of countless miserable expeditions.

"But he really wants to be able to show off the scenery to Leo. Boast a little about our part of Maine."

"I can't think why he should want to do that," Lucinda said shortly. "Who cares if Leo Grosvenor likes it here or not?"

Fran's accent became more aggressively Southern, a sure sign that her stepdaughter was getting on her nerves. "I declare, you are the most *pee*-culiar girl," she said. "Why, everybody in Small Port is just crazy about Leo Grosvenor. Of course we want to show off our little old country to him."

"I don't," Lucinda declared. "I don't give a damn if he likes Small Port or not."

"Well now, you just be nice to him, y'hear?" Fran demanded. "Just because he doesn't strike your particular fancy doesn't mean other girls feel the same."

"You mean Trish has fallen for him." Lucinda had noticed that her stepsister had shown signs of being attracted to their laconic English visitor.

"He's very taken with Trish," Fran announced, and her thin lips tightened. "Besides, it's high time she was married."

Lucinda's big brown eyes widened behind her glasses. "Oh come on, Fran! She's hardly old enough to be left on the shelf." At twenty-four Trish was barely two years older than Lucinda.

"Gina's been married for three whole years," Fran said accusingly, "and they're twins."

"But Gina was practically engaged to Del in kindergarten," Lucinda protested. "You can't use her as an example."

"I'm not using her for any such thing," insisted Fran. "I'm just pointing out that Leo Grosvenor would be a real nice catch for her. He's well-to-do and an English gentleman. So don't you go being rude to him and putting him off the family."

Lucinda bristled. "Rude to him? I've scarcely said two words to the man since he came here."

"That's the point, honey. You just sit around mute as a stone. Glaring."

"Stones don't glare." Lucinda smiled.

"You know what I mean," continued Fran. "I'm not blaming you, Cindy, for lacking the...the social graces. It's not in your character to have charm. But at least make an effort to be pleasant. Having you sit there *glowering* at him must be very disturbing."

The ribbon in Lucinda's light brown hair slipped free, and she retrieved it before saying, "Leo Grosvenor wouldn't be disturbed if I turned into a sea urchin before his very eyes. He doesn't even know I exist." Which was fine, for unlike the rest of her family she was not dazzled by him. She found him arrogant and overbearing, and she was glad those piercing blue eyes of his hardly glanced in her direction.

"If he doesn't notice you it's your own fault," said Fran, changing her tactics. "No man's going to notice a girl who sits and sulks."

"Well, you don't want him to notice me, so there's no problem."

Fran came and stood over her. "Honestly, Cindy! You're so . . . so difficult."

This accusation had been leveled at Lucinda many times. Her mother had died when she was five, and less than a year later Charles Wainwright had married Fran, who was divorced and living in her native Virginia with her twin girls. He and his new wife had wanted Lucinda to call Fran "Mommy," but Lucinda couldn't. The memory of her real mother was too vivid. Her father had been furious. His stepdaughters were eager to call him "Daddy." He couldn't understand Lucinda's reluctance and viewed her bewildered unhappiness as stubbornness. It was decided there and then that Lucinda was "difficult." For years Lucinda had tackled the Mommy problem by not calling Fran anything, and by the time she reached her teens the issue had been dropped.

Fran gave a martyr's sigh and said plaintively, "I've got a date to play squash at the club in half an hour or I'd take you for a walk, get you out in the fresh air instead of straining your eyes over some old book."

"Nice of you, but I spent the morning walking along the cliffs. Right now I have to read. I'm starting *Huckleberry Finn* with my kids this Saturday, and I need to prepare."

Every weekend Lucinda read aloud to a group of children at the library. It was a program she had initiated when she started working there and she loved it, loved sharing her passion for literature with eager young minds, and rediscovering favorite books through their enthusiasm.

"But you're on vacation this week," her stepmother objected. "You should be out-of-doors sailing or something. Toning your body." Instinctively she glanced down at her own taut stomach. "You're the type who runs to fat if you don't work on it. You don't want that ... on top of everything else." Some days Lucinda could chuckle at her stepmother's conviction that to be short and rounded was a disease. "It's too bad you chose such an unhealthy job—being cooped up with all those old books."

"Think of all the exercise I get climbing around the stacks." Lucinda chuckled, an enchanting dimple showing in her cheek.

Fran snorted derisively. "Don't make me laugh, honey. Exercise? You?" She shook her head gloomily. "If ever a girl was born with two left feet ... It would be funny if it wasn't pathetic." Lucinda burrowed down into her chair and pointedly picked up her book, but her stepmother went on. "Maybe you could tear yourself away from that book and give Em a hand in the kitchen. Leo's coming for dinner and I told her to make a cherry pie." She glanced at the watch on her tanned wrist. "Holy Toledo! Look at the time. I declare, Cindy, with all your chatter I'm going to be late for my game."

It was fortunate, Lucinda thought wryly as she closed her book, that two left feet didn't interfere with helping Em run the house. Em certainly didn't get help from any other member of the Wainwright family. Not that Lucinda minded, for she loved Em, who had been with her mother's family before Lucinda was born, and was not so young anymore.

She straightened a picture on her way down the old curved stairs, a lithograph of her father's, taken from a picture he'd painted last year. It was an action piece, a football game. Like all artists Charles Wainwright chose to paint subjects that were close to his heart, but it was not until his agent had suggested he put out a limited edition series of sports pictures that he had made any big money. That particular piece of good fortune had created a new tension in the household.

It had been a matter of great bitterness to Charles that when his first wife died she left the house and its contents to her daughter, to be held in trust until she came of age. He had been furious, but there had been nothing he could do. He still felt resentful, however, and had never forgiven Lucinda's mother for what he considered a last slap at his pride—forcing him to live on Lucinda's "charity."

This was, of course, utter nonsense. Lucinda hadn't a cent, so Charles essentially rented the house, since he paid for all the utilities, maintenance and repairs. But once he had some money in the bank he'd begun pressuring Lucinda to sell him the house. She refused. It might have looked like willful stubbornness to the family, but she had a couple of very good reasons. First, she knew that the moment Fran got her hands on Cliff Top, the house would be modernized and redecorated until every trace of Lucinda's mother was wiped away, and Lucinda couldn't have borne to live there after that.

The other reason was Em. Fran wanted someone young and respectful around the place, not an old woman who had adored the first Mrs. Wainwright and made no bones about the fact that she found the second one inferior. Em would have been fired without a moment's hesitation. And even though Lucinda would have been able to help Em financially with money from the sale, she hadn't the heart to uproot the old lady, take her away from all that was dear and familiar. So she obstinately refused to even discuss the matter.

Her father had been so angry with her that he spent the money he'd put aside for a down payment on *Yankee Doodle*, a sleek racing yacht, the type he'd always yearned for. Lucinda had suggested it might be nice to buy Em a food processor at the same time, but Charles had refused. Instead, he'd taken his family for an expensive skiing holiday in Austria, and had insisted that Lucinda accompany them, which was his way of punishing her, for he knew she was a timorous skier.

Em looked up now from a steaming pot of clam chowder as Lucinda tripped over the doorsill and stumbled into the big old-fashioned kitchen. "Do you think Mr. Grosvenor likes clam chowder?" she asked.

"Who knows or cares! Give it to him anyway. He's lucky to get fed at all."

Em looked doubtful. "I don't fancy givin' folk food they don't like."

"Anyone who doesn't like your clam chowder is a fool." Lucinda's brown eyes glinted. "And who knows, maybe that cap fits Mr. High-and-mighty Grosvenor."

"That one's no fool, for all his fancy accent," the old woman declared firmly. "You have to be pretty smart to get where he is."

Leo Grosvenor was president of a British company of naval architects, which had been started by his grandfather. A well-known naval architect himself, Leo was visiting Small Port as a consultant for the shipbuilding works in town. He'd visited the local art gallery during his stay and had bought a couple of Wainwright lithographs. Charles had happened to be in the gallery at the time, and the two men discovered a mutual interest in sailing. Then Fran arrived and her matchmaking glands started working overtime the minute she clapped eyes on Leo's distinguished six-foot frame. Without more ado she'd invited him for dinner that night. He'd been a frequent visitor ever since.

"Good thing I bought a mess of frozen cherries last month," Em said, putting the lid back on the saucepan. "Mrs. W. wants a pie." She always referred to Fran this way, although Lucinda's mother had always been 'Miss Lillian.'

"I'll make it for you," offered Lucinda, "but I'd better go easy on desserts for a bit. I think I'm gaining weight."

"You don't look any different to me." Em tucked a wisp of silver hair back into her neat bun. "If you're tryin' to look like your stepsisters, forget it! You've got your ma's figure. Nice an' round."

"Nice and out-of-date, you mean," Lucinda grumbled. "Hips and boobs don't go with today's clothes, Em."

"Go naked then," said Em. "You can't go against nature."

Lucinda grinned, showing her pretty white teeth. "Bit too drafty."

"Then stop complainin'." Em made a grab for the sugar bowl when Lucinda hit it with her elbow. "Be careful, child! You're a pretty girl. Just as pretty as Trish or Gina... but in a different way."

"You can say that again!" Morosely Lucinda pushed up her glasses, leaving a floury smudge on her tip-tilted nose. "They don't have to wear glasses, for a start."

"Well, get yourself some of those contact lenses."

"What's the use of that! I'm always either on, or in the sea, and saltwater's no good with contacts." Vehemently she sifted flour into the mixing bowl, so that a fine dust settled over everything.

"No point havin' a tantrum just 'cause you inherited your ma's eyes," said Em, folding her arms and regarding her severely through eyes the color of faded forget-me-nots. "Too bad you didn't inherit her disposition as well."

"Oh, Em, I'm sorry. I didn't mean to be crabby." Lucinda flung down the sifter and put her arms around Em's narrow shoulders. "I'm just in a bad mood because... because of the rain."

Em made a skeptical grunt at the back of her throat. She knew Fran had been upstairs earlier, and she also knew the kind of tactless digs that lady was capable of making. She returned the girl's hug and then said crisply, "You'd better get back to your pastry before you have us both covered in flour."

They worked in silence for a while, and then Em said, "If you want a bit of advice, Lucinda, stop tryin' to please other people all the time. You'll wind up pleasin' no one, least of all yourself."

"You mean I should stop trying to please Dad?" asked Lucinda, starting on the lattice top of her pie.

"Be *yourself* is what I'm tryin' to say," replied the old woman. "Your ma, bless her soul, never tried to be somethin' she wasn't."

Lucinda stopped weaving strips of pastry and looked up, her brown eyes intent. "And was she happy, Em?"

"She was happy enough," Em answered, and then she clamped her jaw tight, because she never gossiped about Miss Lillian's miserable marriage, least of all with Miss Lillian's daughter.

The afternoon was dark for early June, so Em switched on the light and Lucinda's pale brown hair gleamed like a skein of fine silk in the glow. When the pie was baked and the dining room table set, Lucinda went upstairs to shower and change, carefully putting her hair in rollers first. But when she unwound them it still drooped wispily around her face, so she gave up in disgust and merely brushed it till her scalp tingled.

Before deciding what to wear, she padded to the window and stared at the ocean. She had a good view from here of the wide half-moon of Indian Head Beach. It was a great beach for walking, littered with clamshells and streaked in places with silvery chips of mica. She had spent many happy hours there, poking about in rock pools, or watching the antics of eider ducks bobbing in the surf. Her father, who had no patience with anything so aimless, contemptuously called it "Cindy mooning about!"

It was really too dark to see the beach, and she closed the frilled white cotton curtains. She had papered her room with rosebud-sprigged paper in the spring, and sanded and painted the wide planked floor primrose yellow. Her bed was covered with a white cotton spread, gay with multicolored flowers that she'd spent last winter embroidering. All that remained now was to save enough money for a couple of fluffy white rugs, so that her toes wouldn't freeze on cold winter mornings. She loved this airy little room, even if it was in the attic and meant going down to the next floor to use one of the two bathrooms. It was her escape hatch, pretty floral haven that was worth the climb.

She pulled at the sliding door of her closet and examined her wardrobe. She had plenty of clothes, for Fran was generous with her daughters and never bought anything for the twins without buying something for her stepdaughter, too. Which was fine, except few of the garments Fran chose suited Lucinda's round little body. Trish and Gina looked splendid in dresses with big shoulder pads, or hip-hugging tailored jeans. Lucinda didn't. Her little head with its mass of flyaway hair looked like a peanut rising out of those Joan Crawford shoulders, and her full breasts popped the buttons on the masculine type of shirts Fran blessed her with. But every time she wore something she'd bought or made herself, some soft feminine garment that didn't overwhelm her, her father made a fuss because Fran's generosity was being rejected. Because Lucinda wanted so desperately to please him, she would change out of her pretty dress into one of Fran's smart disasters.

With this in mind she chose a new silk dress Fran had given her the week before. It was cut straight with no waist, wide shoulders and a severe neckline. The dress hugged Lucinda's bottom like plaster on a wall, hiding her little waist, making her look bottom-heavy.

Doubtfully she peered at her reflection in the prized Victorian cheval glass. This particular dress seemed worse than usual, and the color, a bright magenta, didn't help. It made her heart-shaped face look like cream cheese. She rubbed more blusher on her cheeks, and applied an extra coating of mascara to her thick lashes. Trish had told her countless times that girls who wore glasses needed to wear lots of eye makeup. In a last effort to soften the severe neckline, she looped her mother's gold locket and chain over her head and tottered from her room on unaccustomed heels.

Her father had come in from his studio and was drinking a beer in the living room. He looked up as his only child came in unsteadily.

"Hi, Dad! Have a good day?"

"Not bad. I started on my Regatta picture." He looked at her over his glass and felt a surge of irritation. "You've got too much rouge on," he said sharply.

She rubbed at her cheeks. "It's this damn dress. The color's too bright."

"It's got nothing to do with the color," he said. And then he added accusingly, "You look more like your mother every day."

She glared at him combatively. "What's wrong with that?"

"Don't get your dander up. She was pretty enough in her way," huffed Charles, "but she had no sense of style, a trait you seem to have inherited. I should have thought you would have learned how to dress from Fran. She's got plenty of style."

"It just so happens that Fran gave me this particular dress," she said icily.

"It's not the dress...."

"Just the person wearing it? Thanks a lot!"

"You don't *carry* clothes the way Fran and Trish do," he persisted. "If you're going to wear fashionable things you have to wear them with panache."

"I guess panache just isn't my style," replied Lucinda wearily. Useless trying to explain to him that although Fran meant well she hadn't any idea how to clothe anybody who was a different physical shape.

"And you're so pale," Charles nagged on. "If you'd get some sun, you wouldn't look as if you'd just crawled out from under a stone."

"It's difficult to get a suntan cooped up in *Yankee Doodle*'s galley," she returned with spirit, for this was an old bone of contention between them. Lucinda had inherited her father's ability to weather even the roughest sea without a suspicion of seasickness, so he insisted she be included in all their sailing trips, for she was invaluable in the galley. She was handy as a crew member, too, but since he barked at her whenever she tripped over a line or dropped something, he succeeded in making her so nervous she became worse than useless. Over the years she had come to hate sailing, but she loved her father and hoped that by persevering she would earn his respect. It hadn't happened yet, but Lucinda was a born optimist.

He dismissed her testily. "You choose to shut yourself up in that library all day. No sun there, either." This was a favorite dig, particularly since Trish taught aerobics at the local athletic club and gave her classes out-of-doors whenever it wasn't raining.

"I walk a lot," Lucinda pointed out.

He gave a contemptuous bark of laughter, for walking was not a recreation he took seriously. "We can be thankful you don't run! You'd be falling over your feet all the time."

Lucinda, her overrouged cheeks a much brighter shade now, said, "Not *all* the time, I wouldn't." But the fight had gone out of her. It was always like this. She did love her father and tried hard to be the kind of daughter he wanted, but all he ever seemed to do was find fault with her.

At that moment Trish stuck her coppery head around the door. "Want another beer, Dad?"

"Thanks, honey," replied Charles, smiling at his stepdaughter and holding out his glass.

"I'll get it," said Lucinda, thankful for an excuse to escape. "Besides, I really should give Em a hand."

"I don't pay Em for you to work in the kitchen," snapped her father, but Lucinda was already out the door.

She kicked off her shoes and left them lying on the floor. "You'd better go and change. Dinner won't be long," she said to Trish, who was wearing a pair of apple-green sweat pants and a bulky white sweater.

"I *am* changed." She took in Lucinda's magenta-clad form. "Where's the party?"

Lucinda groaned inwardly. What an idiot she was! Anyone with half a mind would have realized that a weekday family dinner was a casual affair, but she'd been so eager to please she'd dolled herself up like a Christmas tree.

"*I'll* go up and change then," she told Trish. But just then the doorbell rang, and through the stained glass window they could make out the tall figure of Leo Grosvenor.

"You answer it, Cindy." Trish giggled. "Leo's English. He's probably used to seeing women formally dressed."

"Trish, please! *You* go," Lucinda pleaded, but Trish shook her head, and taking Charles's empty glass from her stepsister, she disappeared in the direction of the kitchen.

Pulling at her skirt, which kept riding up her thighs, Lucinda went to the front door. She opened it just as Leo was about to ring a second time. "Hello!" he said. "I was beginning to wonder if I'd mistaken the night."

"No, of course not." She might not like him, but she had to admit he was impressive to look at. Not exactly handsome—his features were too craggy to be called handsome—but he certainly rated a second glance. Particularly with that shock of silver-gray hair. Seeing his tanned thirtyish face under that frosty thatch always surprised her. The contrast was stunning.

"May I come in?" he asked, for she was blocking the doorway.

"Oh! Sure." She stood aside as he strode into the hall. If he had still been wearing his business suit she would have felt less conspicuous, but he had gone back to his hotel to change into casual slacks and a sport shirt. She cursed under her breath.

"Pardon?" He stared down at her. The hall light made her hair shine like corn silk. Pretty hair, he thought, but her face looked rather odd. She had the look of a little girl who had been experimenting with her mother's makeup. And as for that dress!

She said, "Dad's in the living room. I'll let him know you've arrived," and hurried forward, forgetting that her shoes were lying on the floor. She would have fallen flat on her face if Leo hadn't caught her.

"Are you all right?" he asked, putting her back on her feet.

"Perfectly all right, thank you."

"You're not feeling faint or anything?"

"No." She pulled at her skirt. "I fall over a lot."

"Indeed!" His thick black brows rose a fraction. "Deliberately?"

"Of course not." There was a pause. "I'm badly coordinated."

"Quite a problem."

"I manage," she said coldly. She didn't want Leo Grosvenor patronizing her.

"Not very well, if that demonstration's anything to go by."

"Well enough!" She flung open the door. "Dad! Leo's here," she called, shooting a haughty glare at

Leo before scuttling back to the safety of the kitchen. There she found Trish trying to balance an ice bucket in one hand and a tray of hot cheese canapés in the other.

"Where on earth have you been?" Trish demanded. "I can't find the cocktail napkins anywhere." Lucinda went over to the drawer where they were always kept, took out a handful and put them on the tray. "Is this your idea of dressing down?" her stepsister inquired. "Going without shoes?"

"Do you think I really need to wear high heels with this dress?" asked Lucinda. The way her luck was running this evening she'd be falling over her feet every second step.

Trish nodded her red head. "Absolutely! But you shouldn't wear your glasses, Cindy. Makes you look like a librarian," and she exited swiftly, butting the swinging door with her flat little rump.

"What's the matter with that?" Em commented from the stove. "You *are* a librarian."

"Dowdy she really meant," Lucinda replied glumly. She snatched the offending glasses off her nose and threw them down onto the counter among a jumble of her father's nautical charts.

"Better put those glasses back on. You're blind as a bat without them," cautioned Em.

"Not quite. Things just get fuzzy." And a good thing too, she thought. Now when she caught sight of herself in a mirror, her image would be blurred.

"Don't say I didn't warn you," said Em.

"I won't. Anything I can do?"

"You can go back where you belong—with your father's guest," Em replied firmly.

"They won't miss me."

"Do you want to get me into trouble, Lucinda?"

Lucinda made a comic face. "Okay, you win. But they *won't* miss me, I promise."

And of course she was right. When she'd put her shoes back on and returned to the living room, Fran was there and Charles was enthusiastically telling sailing stories. "...and there we were, hove-to for thirty-six hours, with Fran and the girls as sick as dogs," Charles finished happily.

Lucinda remembered that jaunt well...too well! She remembered heating cans of consommé in the swaying galley for her green-faced stepsisters, and trying to tempt Fran with crackers. It had been thirty-six hours of hell.

"Do you have a boat back home?" Fran asked, eyeing Leo reflectively.

"I have two. One for cruising and one for racing."

"*Do* you!" said Fran, and Lucinda felt herself go hot. Only a fool could have missed the gleam of acquisitiveness in her stepmother's eyes.

Then Em rang the old ship's bell to call them to dinner. As they trooped into the dining room Fran drew Leo aside. "Charles and I are planning to send Trish on a little visit to England next spring," she confided, "but she doesn't know a soul over there." She smiled archly. "It would take such a weight off my mind, knowing that you were looking after my little girl."

"I'm sure an attractive girl like Trish won't be without friends for long," said Leo diplomatically. "If I'm around I'll be happy to show her my part of Sussex, of course, but I am out of the country a great deal."

He was a smooth customer, all right, thought Lucinda. And what was all this about sending Trish to England? Fran must have thought that one up on the spur of the moment. She was being so blatant, Lucinda could imagine Leo telling his English cronies when he got home about this pushy Southern belle and her relentless matchmaking. He pulled out Fran's chair before sitting in his own seat, which was, of course, beside Trish, and Lucinda glared over at him fuzzily. Even if Fran was sometimes tactless and hurtful, she was part of the Wainwright family, and Lucinda wasn't having any snooty Brit look down his beaky nose at her.

Em put a bowl of steaming chowder in front of her, and still frowning, she picked up her spoon and dipped it into the milky broth.

"Do you have a very la-arge house in England, Leo?" cooed Fran.

"Well it's not Buckingham Palace," Leo said, crumbling chowder crackers, "just a small manor house."

"A manor house," exclaimed Trish. "How dreamy!"

"Especially in winter when the pipes freeze," he said, and then he looked straight across at Lucinda and smiled at her. She was so startled that she ducked her head and her locket fell with a plop into her soup, splashing the front of her dress.

"What in God's name are you doing?" snapped her father as she sucked excess chowder from it before drying it on her napkin.

"Cleaning my jewelry." She was conscious of Leo, grinning broadly at the opposite side of the table.

"Honestly, Cindy!" said Fran with a little trill of laughter. She turned to Leo. "I'm afraid Cindy is just the clumsiest thing alive. You must excuse her."

"That's nothing," said Trish, joining in the fun, "remember the time we went skiing and Cindy fell over when she was standing still at the bottom of the hill."

"Oh my stars yes!" gurgled Fran. "We'd just done a run and we were lining up for the tow when Cindy fell—crash—for no reason."

Lucinda, always the good sport, joined in their laughter. No point explaining that she'd fallen because her legs were still weak from fear after that terrifying slope.

"My daughter takes after my late wife," Charles informed his guest. "She was also hopeless at athletics."

"Poor old Cindy can't even get off a boat without skinning her shins," Trish said gaily, and proceeded to tell Leo about the time Lucinda leaped off *Yankee Doodle*, misjudged the distance and landed on all fours on the concrete dock.

Still smiling, although by now she felt as if the corners of her lips were being held up by Scotch Tape, Lucinda started collecting the empty soup bowls.

"It must give you great satisfaction," Leo said, as she reached for his bowl, "to be such a source of amusement to your family." His eyes were totally expressionless, like blank pieces of bright blue glass.

And what was that supposed to mean? A form of snide British humor, she decided, and favoring Leo with a glare, went into the kitchen.

Before returning to the dining room she replaced her glasses. Useless worrying whether they looked wrong with her dress or not. The dress was hideous anyway, as well as being liberally splashed with chowder. She had tried wiping at her front with a damp dishtowel, but was not at all sure the resulting damp patch looked much better.

Disheartened, she returned to the dining room in time to help pass the vegetables. The family had mercifully dropped the hilarious topic of Lucinda's general awkwardness and were all listening to Leo, who was answering a question Fran had just put to him.

"I took over the firm when my father retired, just eighteen months ago," he was saying. "He'd always wanted to settle in the west and golf and garden—his two passions—so when the doctors told him to slow down because of his heart, he bought a house in Devon and left me to run things."

"And do you like it?" Charles asked. "Do you like designing ships?"

Leo cut a slice of meat loaf and put it on his fork. "I enjoy my work very much. I like anything to do with the sea. That's why I live in Sussex." He kept his fork in his left hand to eat, not putting down his knife the way Americans did. *Affected,* thought Lucinda unfairly, as she speared her broccoli.

Fran leaned toward him confidentially. "And what's Sussex like, compared to here?"

"Different. Softer countryside. Maine's rugged."

"Maine's wild and rocky shore," Lucinda muttered under her breath.

Leo said, *"Very* rocky. Quite a forbidding coastline."

She tilted her chin defiantly, instantly on the defensive. "I think it's beautiful."

"So do I. Forbidding things can be very beautiful. I'm very taken with Small Port, and the history of the whole area fascinates me."

"I thought only the British had a history," said Lucinda, unable to stop herself from goading him.

"We sometimes recognize other people's," he replied, eyes frigid. "I think America has her share of past. The area around here was settled in the 1700s, wasn't it? That seems to me to be pretty historic."

"Some people believe that Norse explorers came along this coast long before that," said Lucinda, unable to suppress the eagerness in her voice. "Rock carvings have been found at Damariscove Island, and rune stones on the shore of Spirit Pond at Popham."

"For heaven's sake, don't start on your old history," said Trish with a groan. She leaned toward Leo, a copper wave falling across her forehead. "Local history's an obsession with her. Give it a rest, Cindy, and don't be a bore," she implored.

Lucinda bit her lip. She supposed she was boring. But when she worked on a library exhibition of local history for the chamber of commerce last year, she had found it fascinating and had read everything she could lay her hands on. She had always felt that the history of Small Port was as much a part of her as her bones, that her roots clung to the land as tenaciously as the roots of the dark fir trees on the shore.

By the time they reached the coffee stage, Trish's sister, Gina, and her husband arrived. Del eyed the empty pie plate ruefully. "What kind was it?" he asked Em, who had just deposited the cream and sugar on the table.

"Cherry." She picked up the empty dish and started for the kitchen.

"Did Cindy make it?" Em nodded, and he groaned to Lucinda, "My favorite and you didn't save me a piece."

"Didn't want you to get fat. Got to preserve your boyish figure," Lucinda teased. She was fond of her brother-in-law, although they had nothing in common. The only things Del ever read were manuals on sailing and the sports pages of the newspaper, but this hefty young man of twenty-four had a heart as big as all outdoors. He reminded Lucinda of a friendly, oversize puppy.

"I didn't know it was a formal evening," said Gina, eyeing Lucinda's dress.

Lucinda flushed. "I wanted to wear the new dress Fran gave me." Gina always made her feel a fool. She had since they were children. She was the prettier of the twins—and the colder. Trish might tease thoughtlessly, but Gina teased to wound. Now she gave Leo her cool social smile.

"I'm sorry the weather's so lousy for you," she said. Her hair, which was the same coppery shade as her sister's, and which, unlike Trish, she wore shoulder length, fell in a heavy curve on either side of her face. Lucinda had tried to train her silky hair to do the same, but all she'd ever achieved was a series of strands that got in her eyes and mouth.

"Rain isn't unknown in England." Leo smiled back politely, but his smile didn't reach his eyes.

"I can't wait for you to try out *Yankee Doodle*," Charles said, helping himself to sugar. "I'm tied up this weekend. Maybe we could fix it for the weekend after?"

Leo took a sip of coffee—black with nothing in it, Lucinda noticed. "I'm sorry but I'm afraid that won't be possible. I'll be back in England then."

Fran's head jerked up. "So soon?"

"I've finished here earlier than I expected. I'm flying to New York Sunday night to tie up a few loose ends before taking the Concorde home."

"I really wanted to be along when you tried out my boat, but I can't duck out of this weekend," Charles explained gloomily. "Fran and I are going to Boston on business. I guess Trish will have to crew for you."

"Well, that won't be the end of the world," Fran commented, her green eyes knowing.

Trish said, "Mom, you've forgotten! I'm playing in the squash tournament this weekend."

"Cancel it!" snapped Fran.

"I can't," her daughter objected, "it's too late to get a replacement."

"It's hardly imperative that I sail your husband's boat," Leo interjected his face wooden.

Charles and Fran were beginning to make Lucinda feel sick with shame, clamoring at their guest like this. "I'd really set my heart on your opinion of my boat," explained Charles. "Maybe Del and Gina . . . ?"

Gina dashed his hopes by saying firmly, "Sorry, Dad, Del and I have to go to Boothbay to show a new line of sailboards." Del and Gina helped his father run a large sporting goods store in town, and their weekends were often spent demonstrating merchandise.

"My opinion really isn't worth all this fuss," Leo insisted, his lips set in a thin line. But he underestimated his host's determination. Once Charles had set his heart on something he would do everything in his power to get his way. Acquiring *Yankee Doodle* had been a high point in his life. He had dreamed for years of owning a racing yacht. Now he wanted to be able to boast to his friends that this British nautical designer—this "expert"—had sailed it and declared it a winner, and he wasn't about to be cheated. He took a deep breath.

"Well," he said, "there's nothing else for it. Lucinda will have to crew for you."

CHAPTER TWO

LUCINDA'S INITIAL REACTION was to flatly refuse, but then she changed her mind. She wasn't going to let a stranger witness a family tiff.

"We'll have to go on the afternoon tide," she said curtly. "I'm busy in the morning."

"So am I." His blue eyes were glacial. "We don't need to make an all-day expedition of it."

"Perish the thought!" she said and then because she wasn't naturally rude, added, "The weather isn't nice enough." But this tall Englishman stirred an antagonism in her that she seemed incapable of controlling. When Leo turned his insolent blue gaze in her direction she felt all her hackles rise.

As soon as they returned to the living room she excused herself and went upstairs. She yanked the magenta dress over her head and flung it to the back of her closet. She would never wear it again. She might want to please her father, but there were limits. She had already sacrificed her Saturday afternoon walk over the cliffs, and now was trapped into taking Leo out on *Yankee Doodle* instead.

She heard Leo's car drive off as she padded down to the bathroom to brush her teeth. Trish was already there, rubbing cleansing lotion onto her face. "Thought I'd get an early night," she said. "Got to be on form for the tournament."

Lucinda squeezed toothpaste onto her brush. "We've all got to be on form," she said morosely, thinking how frisky *Yankee Doodle* was going to be if the wind didn't let up.

"Poor old Leo!" remarked Trish. "Little does he know what he's in for."

"At least I won't be sick all over him," Lucinda returned, unusually truculent.

Thoughtfully wiping her face with a tissue, Trish said, "What's bugging, you Cindy?"

"Sorry!" said her stepsister through a mouthful of toothpaste. "I wish you were going with Leo. He'd much rather have you around."

"If he craves my company so much, why doesn't he come and see me play?"

"Do you mind very much? Fran was saying earlier that you two were..."

"An item?" Trish pushed past her to get to the basin. "Not yet. He seemed interested for a while, but nothing came of it."

"But what about you?" Lucinda persisted. "Are you interested?"

"That depends." The redhead splashed cold water on her face, then patted it dry. "If Mom really does send me to England, I sure mean to case out that manor house of his."

Her expression was decidedly mercenary, and Lucinda drew her delicate brows together in a frown. "What's that got to do with it?"

"Don't be dumb! Once I see where and how he lives, I'll know for sure whether he's worth going after."

"You mean because of his money?" cried Lucinda, shaken by such nonchalant greed.

"You know your trouble, Cindy?" Trish patted cream onto her tanned skin. "You read too many books."

"But what about love?" Lucinda's soft brown eyes glowed. "You can't fall in love with a man just because he's rich."

Trish gave a chuckle. "Wanna bet?"

Lying in bed that night, Lucinda could almost find it in her heart to feel sorry for Leo, being so relentlessly pursued by both mother and daughter, but then she remembered those chill blue eyes of his and that obstinate jut of chin. A man with a chin like that certainly didn't need sympathy.

THE RAIN HAD STOPPED, but the weather had not really improved. The sky was filled with tatters of dark cloud and, if anything, the wind seemed stronger.

Lucinda went downstairs early and found her father already in the kitchen, listening to the weather report. "Too bad Leo has to leave tomorrow," he said, flicking off the radio. "It sounds like terrific sailing for a bit."

"You mean it's going to clear up?"

"I mean it's going to be real sailing weather. None of your panty-waist cruising." He stared challengingly, knowing that cruising in fair weather was the only kind of sailing Lucinda enjoyed. She thought wistfully that it would have been nice if he showed some gratitude, since she was giving up her Saturday.

Her reading group that morning was something of a trial. With the bad weather there were more children at the library than usual, and a number of these were restless and didn't want to hear about Huckleberry Finn. Finally Lucinda was forced to exert her authority and point out that the regulars had voted for Mr. Twain, and if the casuals didn't like it they could leave. They settled down after that, but she still had to keep on top of things, and by the time she drove home for lunch she had a headache.

One hour and two Aspirins later Leo arrived. Lucinda had only just changed from her print skirt into jeans and sweater when Em called up the stairs, "Mr. Grosvenor's waitin' in his car, Lucinda. Says there's no point in him comin' in."

Cursing him for being prompt, she grabbed her eyeglass cord—a precaution against dropping her glasses overboard—and ran downstairs, tying back her hair as she went. He had given her no time to put on even a dab of lipstick, not that she supposed it mattered. This was hardly a date.

He hadn't even turned off the engine of his car, and was sitting staring ahead as if the sooner he got this obligation over with the better. Seeing his tight jaw, Lucinda was of half a mind to suggest he simply take a look over *Yankee Doodle* and forget about the sail, but remembering how much her father wanted Leo to find out how the boat handled stopped her.

"Good afternoon," she said brightly as she clambered into the passenger seat. "You're certainly on time."

He said shortly, "No point hanging about."

"No point at all," she agreed, her hackles standing on end like porcupine quills. She clamped her lips tight until they arrived at the marina.

It was just a small concrete dock built in a local farmer's meadow that ran down to the river. There were two other boats bobbing about on the choppy water, but they were like jetsam compared to Charles Wainwright's trim craft, a thirty-two-foot racing sloop, painted light blue, her brightwork gleaming even in this dull light.

"Very nice. Very nice indeed," murmured Leo, his eyes not quite so chill. "Let's put this baby through her paces, shall we?" Nodding, Lucinda watched him leap on board with the agility of a mouflon.

She threw her canvas ditty bag onto the deck and gritted her teeth. Getting on and off any boat was always a problem for Lucinda, and *Yankee Doodle*'s lethal double guardrail was an added hazard. When her father had first purchased her, Lucinda had tentatively suggested that a small gangplank might be a good idea, but this had been greeted with such derision she'd never mentioned it again.

Now she took a deep breath and hurled herself across the black water. She landed on the outside of the rails and nearly lost her balance. Leo reached out a hand and hauled her over.

"Thanks," she muttered through dry lips. Fishing keys out of her bag, she promptly dropped them and he picked them up for her. "Thanks," she muttered again, and unlocking the cabin door, she led the way below.

Yankee Doodle's berths were blue canvas and matched her paint; the two-ring Primus stove in the galley was clean and sparkling, and the radio navigation equipment was the latest model.

"I'll just put on my foul-weather stuff," she said, going to the locker for her yellow Gore-Tex suit, which hung with the rest of the family's gear.

Leo pulled an elegant navy zip-up suit from the bag he'd brought on board. "I even remembered to bring my boots," he said, waggling a pair of rather large rubber waders at her.

She smiled thinly. There was something uncomfortably intimate about suiting up together like this.

"Where can I stow this?" He held out his smart black leather jacket, and she took it as if it might burn her fingers and slipped it awkwardly over the hanger that had held her suit.

"Mind if I look around before we get under way?" he asked.

"Go ahead." She went to the galley to check that there was instant coffee and powdered milk, while he moved around, examining the navigational equipment and checking over the sails in the locker.

"Your father's certainly done himself proud," he commented when he'd finished.

"Yeah! And Em's still chopping vegetables by hand."

Slightly mystified, he said, "Pardon?"

"Nothing." She pushed back a straying wisp of hair. "Ready to go?"

"Certainly." He smiled, and she thought he should do that more often. *He looks almost human when he smiles.*

She started the engine without any difficulty and left it in neutral while Leo cast off, thankful that he'd undertaken that task without being asked. They were under power for this part of the trip, and she stayed at the tiller while he went below to listen to a weather report, only passing the tiller to him when he returned on deck.

"Not very promising," he told her, "but at least no fog. I think we should head west, stay around the Casco Bay area." Although he'd made it sound as if she had a say in the decision, she was too used to sailing with autocratic captains not to recognize an order when she heard it.

She hoped he was also taking in the scenery while they cruised, since it had seemed important to her father that their guest admire it. This particular stretch of river was a favorite of hers. It was dotted with islands, some linked to the mainland by bridges, some inhabited only by seabirds. The spire of a white clapboard church poked out of a thicket of conifers, and on a reedy inlet close by was tethered a tiny yellow

seaplane, bobbing up and down like an agitated but-
terfly. As they approached the mouth of the river they
started meeting the swell coming in from the ocean.

"Quite a sea running," Leo said gleefully. "There's
more wind than I thought. Luckily it's dead on shore,
so let's get some sail up here. I think we'll start with
some reef in the main."

"There's a dogleg in the river where it goes around
the promontory," she said and he smiled, for like all
born sailors the more difficult the challenge the better
he liked it.

He put *Yankee Doodle* onto automatic pilot, and
Lucinda helped him hoist the jib and the main. When
she performed these tasks with her father, he shouted
at her so often and made her feel like such a fool that
she became all thumbs and botched even the simplest
job. But Leo didn't shout. His orders were compre-
hensible and delivered with crisp authority. She actually got through the ordeal with hardly a qualm,
while he maneuvered the yacht around the jagged
rocks, handling the boat with ease. He was that necessary mixture of relaxation and alertness, and *Yankee Doodle* slipped through the turn like a knife
through butter.

Once they were out in the open sea, he cut the engine and put the yacht on course. "Terrific!" he cried,
as the wind filled her sails. "Tell your father she flies
like a bird."

Lucinda nodded and hung on tight. *Yankee Doodle*
was heeled over, plunging through the green water like
a dolphin. Leo's pure delight in the tearing wind and

blinding spray was infectious, and to her considerable surprise she found she was actually enjoying herself.

As they went on the wind freshened. "We'd better take more reef in the main," shouted Leo happily. "Take the tiller when I've come into the wind."

This was a part of sailing that Lucinda hated. She knew it was perfectly safe, but she disliked bouncing around like a cork, particularly since it was generally about this time that her female relatives got seasick. But today she was crewing for someone who was as far removed from seasickness as she was, and the yacht's antics didn't seem to bother her nearly as much.

When she handed the tiller back to him, their hands touched briefly. His were cold as ice and her first instinct was to chafe and warm them, the way Em used to do for her when she was little. Hastily she jammed her hands into her pockets. "How about a cup of coffee?" she suggested gruffly. "Warm us up."

"Good idea." He smiled. "You're looking a mite frozen."

With the wind raking his hair back off his face he looked positively boyish, and without thinking she blurted, "How old are you, anyway?"

He laughed, and all the stern lines on his face softened. "Are you implying that I'm too old to be messing about in borrowed boats?"

"Of course not. It's just that...with your hair...it's hard to guess your age." She flushed. "Not that it's any of my business, of course."

"I'm thirty-three. My hair is simply the result of a misspent youth." He grinned. "Gray hair runs in my family. My father was gray by the time he was twenty-five."

"Were you gray at twenty-five, too?"

"Twenty-four. I beat him by one year." He pulled up the hood of his jacket. "How about that coffee?"

Waiting for the kettle to boil, she reflected that this afternoon could have been a lot worse. Not that she liked Leo Grosvenor any better, in spite of that newly discovered smile of his. She poured hot water over the coffee crystals. Black for him, she remembered. Perhaps this trip wasn't quite the calamity she had foreseen. Soon they would be home, and she could get on with her life and forget Leo Grosvenor even existed.

When she returned, the wind had become stronger and she skidded across the wet deck as if she were wearing skates. Fortunately the coffee mugs were the lidded kind, with a spout for drinking, otherwise she would have spilled the lot. Leo was looking serious.

"It seems to be blowing into a storm," he said. "I'll check on the weather again. You take over here for a bit." He disappeared down the hatch, coffee forgotten, leaving Lucinda to cling to the tiller, which seemed intent on tearing itself out of her hands. Her new-found sense of enjoyment started to fade.

The sky was a threatening mass of purple clouds, and the wind shrieked through the rigging like a banshee. Then the first really big wave broke over the boat and water streamed down the deck, while *Yankee Doodle* pitched and shuddered like a terrier shaking water from its coat. Blinded by the saltwater that had splashed over her glasses, Lucinda blearily stared at the compass needle and desperately tried to keep on course.

Leo returned and took the tiller from her numb hands. "We're in for a storm."

"You don't say," she gasped as another wave swamped them.

"There's no way I'm going to risk going through that turn at the river mouth with the wind in this quarter, so we'll have to make port somewhere else and sit it out."

"That could be hours," she squealed.

He ignored her dismay. "I know roughly where we are, but I'm not sure where we should head for. Any ideas?"

She bit her lip and tasted salt. "Marshall's Island. It's about twenty miles south of Small Port. It's supposed to have a good harbor."

"Go below and mark it on the chart," he ordered, "then come back here and I'll lay the course while you steer."

Taking the two mugs of untouched coffee with her, she stumbled back to the cabin and put them in the sink. *Yankee Doodle* was pitching so hard she had to cling to every available surface to reach the chart table. Finally she found Marshall's Island and marked it with a wobbly cross.

She took a quick look out the porthole. They were in the trough of a wave, and all she could see was a shining wall of water that hurled itself over them. The water poured over the transom like a miniature Niagara Falls.

Back on deck she crawled on her hands and knees toward the stern. Leo paid no attention to this unorthodox method of locomotion; he merely yelled, "Hang on tight to the tiller. I'll be as quick as I can."

He was, too, but it still seemed a long time and Lucinda had trouble holding the bucking yacht on course. She was also wet and cold. Her foul-weather suit had never fitted well; water tended to seep in between her chin and the hood, and icy trickles were now creeping down her body.

He returned and told her that they should reach the island in a couple of hours. "Go below and fetch a couple of safety harnesses. On the double!" he barked when she hesitated, and she crawled back across the treacherous deck and fell into the swaying cabin.

Here she found the coffee mugs rolling around in the sink like marbles. The door to the locker where the food was stored had burst open, too, spilling its contents over the floor. With difficulty she collected everything, and then just as she was about to batten down the cupboard door, a particularly large wave broke over the yacht, flinging open the door again and spilling the carefully stowed contents.

"Oh God, *no*!" cried Lucinda. She'd forgotten to close the hatches! Water gushed in and swirled around the cabin, before rushing down the drain holes to the bilge. A box of rice burst open and mingled with a soaking package of cereal. Raisins and dates were scattered across the wet floor like grain. Something else was tangled wetly around her legs, too. Cautiously she picked it up—Leo's jacket dripped heavily from her hands. She couldn't have put it on the hanger securely enough when they boarded.

Didn't seawater do awful things to leather? Make it stiff as a board and streak it with unremovable stains? She flung the sodden thing into a berth and lashed it down. This wasn't the time to worry about it. More water was pouring in. At this rate *Yankee Doodle* wouldn't be dried out for days, and her father would be livid. Grabbing two safety harnesses from the locker, she battled her way back on deck, making sure this time that the hatches were securely fastened.

"What did you do, have a nap down there?" asked Leo sourly.

"There was a lot to clear up." She decided this was not the moment to break the news about his jacket. She passed him his harness and pulled on her own, clipping herself to the guardrail. Then she waited for fear to clutch at her throat. She always felt fear when she was wearing a safety harness, which was irrational, but she couldn't help it. She had lost a grandfather and an uncle at sea, and death by drowning was all she could think of when she was fastened to the boat like this. So she set her chattering teeth, clung to a winch with all her might and waited for the nightmare voyage to end.

It seemed endless. She was so weary she fell into a kind of catatonic trance, conscious of only the battering wind and the roar and hiss of the sea. She must have finally drifted off into an uneasy sleep, only to wake with a jerk when she fell sideways against Leo.

"S-sorry." She blinked myopically into the gathering dusk. "Is it getting calmer?"

"No," he said shortly, "but it's time you roused yourself. We're coming to the island. I'll need you to give me a hand to moor."

She was so cold and tired when they finally reached the little harbor she wasn't sure she would have the strength to hold the lines. She managed it, however, only tearing a fingernail in the process.

Leo glared at two dilapidated fishing boats tied up at the peeling dock. Apart from them and a huddle of disconsolate gulls, Marshall's Island seemed to be deserted. Grim-faced, he led the way to the reeking cabin below.

"This happened when you forgot to close the hatch, I take it."

Miserably she nodded, attempting to pick up some grains of rice with salt-puckered fingers.

"Oh leave it, leave it!" he said irritably. "You can clean up later. We can't stay in this mess anyway, we'll have to go into the village."

"Into the village!" She gave a humorless snort. "This is a small rock in the Atlantic, not a tourist resort!"

He looked at her with active dislike. "We can't wait out the storm down here. It's as chill as the grave."

It was then she noticed he was shaking with the cold and his elegant long fingers were numb and white where they had gripped the tiller. She didn't want him coming down with pneumonia, so she said, "I think there's some rum in the galley. You'd better have a tot.''

She found the rum and poured him a generous ration, and he knocked it back in one swallow. It was dark in the cabin, but even in the gloom he looked uncomfortably pale, his face drawn with fatigue.

"That's better," he said, putting the empty glass in the sink. "Now, let's get out of here." He started for the locker. "Where's my jacket?"

"Er...um...it's here," gulped Lucinda, pointing to the berth.

He examined it briefly. "Marvelous!"

"Maybe you'd better go on wearing your foul-weather gear till it dries," she suggested meekly.

"Frankly, I doubt if it will ever dry," he said coldly. "Let's see if you've destroyed my money, too." He felt in an inner pocket and pulled out a wet leather wallet. "Limp but acceptable, I think." He counted through a pile of damp bills.

"Oh, good!" said Lucinda with a fatuous smile.

"Too bad I left my passport back at the hotel. Think what fun you could have had throwing that into the sea.''

"I didn't do it on purpose," she protested, stung by his sarcasm.

"That's the excuse all incompetent people use," he replied cuttingly.

Back on deck he leaped off *Yankee Doodle* without even bothering to see if she was following him. So much for English gallantry, she thought, as she clumsily hauled herself off the boat and trailed after him up the hill.

A handful of houses clung to the side of the cliff, and the ground floor of one of these had been turned into a general store of sorts. A dim light showed through the grimy windows. Leo knocked and then pushed open the door, Lucinda on his heels. The sudden warmth of the musty little room misted her glasses, so that she walked into a stand holding out-of-date postcards and sent it flying. Views of Casco Bay spilled to the floor.

"You've successfully wrecked the cabin, isn't that enough for you?" inquired Leo.

"I can't see!" she snapped, trying to pick up postcards with frozen fingers.

A plump girl came out of the back room. "Where'd you folks come from?"

While Leo explained their situation, Lucinda shoved the cards back into their stand, taking angry peeks at him all the while. She had never known such a sarcastic brute. She hated him. *Hated* him! To be stranded on this godforsaken island with him was the last straw!

" . . . so we're on the horns of a dilemma," Leo finished saying.

The girl regarded him blankly. "On the horns of a *what*?"

"He means we're in a jam," said Lucinda, coming up to the counter. "He talks that way. He's English."

"I figured that." The girl grinned. "Sounds cute. Like on television."

Leo fixed her with a look of stone. "Is there likely to be a boat going to the mainland?" he asked.

"Not tonight there ain't."

"I have a plane to catch tomorrow."

"Not in this storm. It'll likely have cleared by morning. Meanwhile you'll just have to stay on your boat."

"That is not possible," said Leo, speaking slowly and distinctly, as if to a backward child. "The yacht is not equipped for sleeping. Besides—" he gave Lucinda a murderous glance "—it's soaking wet."

"Stay in the motel then," the girl said stolidly.

"Motel! What motel?" asked Lucinda.

The girl jerked her head. "In back. We got two units, but one's being used for storage right now."

"I'm not spending the night in a motel with him," said Lucinda, horrified.

"Don't screech," Leo commanded. "Face facts. We don't have a choice."

Lucinda appealed to the girl. "Couldn't we be put up separately? Maybe someone has room in their cottage?"

The girl shook her head. "Folks here got no room for overnight visitors."

"Since it bothers my...*companion*...so much, perhaps I could sleep in the unit that's being used for storage," Leo suggested.

The girl picked up a dishcloth and wiped it over the counter in lazy circles. "No way! It's plumb full of Granddad's lobster pots, an' fishing gear an' stuff." She looked at them and giggled. "There's a pullout sofa bed in the cabin as well as the regular bed. You could use that."

"That's it then!" He raked his fingers through his hair and turned to Lucinda. "You'll be perfectly safe," he assured her coldly, peeling some damp bills from his wallet to pay for the motel.

She said, "I'll send you my share when I get home."

He looked gloomy. "If we ever do."

She didn't bother to reply. This would be the first time she had spent the night with a man. It was a hideous trick of fate that it would be a sexless, loveless night, spent in the company of a man she detested.

CHAPTER THREE

BEFORE THEY WENT to the cabin they were served an unappetizing meal cooked on a stove that looked as if it hadn't been cleaned since it was installed.

The girl slapped two hamburgers in front of them. Leo poked at the greasy patty. "What is this exactly?"

"A hamburger. You can't expect Cordon Bleu here," said Lucinda briskly.

"Cordon Bleu! This looks as if it's made of plastic!" The girl dropped a tea bag into a mug and ran hot water from the tap over it. "What on earth are you doing?" he asked her.

Lucinda snapped, "She's making your tea."

"She's not making anything remotely like tea." He shuddered down at the mug. "It looks like a drowned mouse."

The girl giggled nervously. "I'll just go and check on the towels in the cabin," she said, edging out of the door.

"My last night in Maine I had planned to feast on lobster and Californian Chablis," Leo muttered.

Lucinda hunched her shoulders. "You're not the only one whose weekend is wrecked."

"It's not a case of wreckage," he growled. "You seem to forget I have a plane to catch."

"So you might miss a business appointment." She attempted a sneer. "Big deal!"

"Not business, as a matter of fact." His eyes glinted. "Strictly pleasure."

So, he was meeting a woman in New York! Good luck to her. Personally Lucinda would prefer dating a hyena. "How do you know *I'm* not missing a date?" she asked, certain he assumed that she was never asked out.

"I don't, but I think it most unlikely."

"Do you!" She was right, the swine clearly considered her a social failure.

"Otherwise you'd have mentioned it before."

"I hope you don't imagine I'm enjoying myself," she snarled. "I'd rather be . . . be cleaning the oven . . . than spending time with you."

His eyes were like cold blue neon and she felt a frisson of alarm, but he remained silent and after an angry pause she turned her shoulder to him and attacked her soggy hamburger.

When the girl came back and told them that the cabin was ready, Lucinda asked if the island was connected to the mainland by phone. Upon learning that it was, she appealed to Leo to lend her the money to call home. "Em will be frantic," she said.

"You don't have to pay for the call," said the girl. "Have it on the house. The phone's in Granddad's office."

Lucinda had some difficulty locating the phone in the jumble of tinned goods and assorted groceries that littered the "office." Eventually she found it nestling under a pile of paper towels and dialed the mainland. When Em came on the line she seemed remarkably unperturbed. "Aren't you worried at all?" Lucinda asked, a trifle put out by such resolute calm.

"There's no point worryin'," Em said. "Mr. Grosvenor knows how to manage a boat. You're in capable hands."

"I just hope his capable hands don't wander. I'm sharing a room with him tonight."

"He won't touch you," Em said. "Unless you want him to."

"There's no chance of that!" squeaked Lucinda.

"I don't know. He's nice enough lookin'."

"So is deadly nightshade," observed Lucinda, hanging up.

The motel looked suspiciously like a converted garden shed. As she approached it an old man—granddad presumably—came out.

"He—" he jerked a scaly thumb in the direction of the cabin "—he sez you gotta have extra sheets on account of you're goin' to use the sofa bed." He gave a leer. "Things has sure changed since I was a young 'un."

Lucinda's eyes turned from warm brown velvet to chill autumnal russet. "This is an emergency, not a wild weekend."

Granddad merely cackled evilly.

"Dirty old man!" she muttered, opening the door to the cabin and colliding with a chair.

"Do you think you could manage to take two consecutive steps without crashing into the furniture?" said Leo, who's mood had clearly worsened.

"My glasses are covered in salt, I can't *see*." She rubbed at her barked shins.

"Salt has nothing to do with it. You're hopelessly inept." He switched on the rickety bedside lamp and glared. "I think they use glowworms for light bulbs in this dump. It's about as bright as a disused coal mine."

"I wasn't planning to read in bed," said Lucinda, scuttling into the bathroom. "How's the hot water situation?"

"The 'ancient mariner' assures me there's plenty." He came to the bathroom door, which was so low he was forced to stoop. "You can use the shower first."

"You bet I will!" She would *wallow* under the shower, get really warm. It would serve him right if she used up all the hot water.

She washed her glasses and wiped them dry with a piece of toilet paper. He was right, it *was* dim in here. They must use five-watt bulbs. Then she caught sight of herself in the mirror and wished it were dimmer. Her eyes were red-rimmed, her lips swollen and cracked. But it was her hair that was the worst. Lankly plastered to her head and rime-white with salt, it made her look like an albino mouse!

She peeled off her foul-weather suit and started to remove her wet sweater when a thought struck her.

Hastily pulling the sweater on again, she went to the door. Leo was struggling with the pullout bed.

"What will I wear to sleep in?" she asked.

He let go of the bed, and when it crashed shut with a clang he swore explicitly. "Did you bring a nightie with you?"

"Of course not."

"Then I suggest you sleep in your underwear if it's dry enough. Failing that—your skin!" He tossed the cotton bedspread at her. "You can use this as a dressing gown if you're feeling shy."

"I'm not shy, I'm cold," she grumbled, taking the spread into the bathroom, although she did feel rather shy at the thought of parading in front of him in her bra and panties. Not that he would give her a second glance, of course. Glamorous willowy girls, like Trish, were more in his line, not small, plump ones, who fell over their own feet.

The water smelled peculiar but there was plenty of it and it was hot, and although the only soap available was the remains of a yellow bar that seemed to have done service in the kitchen, she enjoyed a long lathery shower.

When she had dried herself she wrapped the bedspread around her shoulders. There was a loud crash from the other room and cautiously she peered around the door. Leo was still fighting with the pull-out bed, which had clamped shut, bedclothes squeezing out from either side like a filling of a squashed sandwich.

"What on earth are you doing?"

"Bloody thing! The mechanism's rusted, it won't stay folded out." He aimed a kick at it. "We'll have to share the bed. This thing's worse than useless."

She squeaked, "Share the bed?" He pushed both hands through his rumpled hair till it stood on end like an iron crown. "What else do you suggest?" He pointed to the only other piece of furniture that the cabin possessed—a wooden kitchen chair.

"I could sleep on *top* of the sofa bed," she suggested.

"It's not flat enough to sit on, let alone lie on. You can barricade yourself with the extra bedclothes if you're worried." He yanked at the trapped sheets. The sofa relinquished them with a sound of tearing cloth. "Here! I'm going to have my shower."

Alone in the room, she hung her damp clothes over various nails that were poking through the wooden walls and then wrapped herself up in one of the extra blankets. Crawling into the bed, she lay on the extreme edge and pulled the blanket up over her head. The rough material tickled her skin so she couldn't relax into a comfortable position. She could hear the water running in the shower, and again she cursed fate, and miserably scratched her thigh, trying to wriggle a nest for herself in the lumpy mattress. Leo turned off the shower and she squeezed her eyes tight shut. Better pretend to be asleep. She didn't fancy bandying any more insults.

He walked around to her side of the bed, and she opened her eyes a fraction to find out what he was up to. Through the screen of her long lashes she saw him pull the curtains shut. He wore a towel around his waist and nothing else. She forgot her dislike for a moment in admiration. His tanned skin was smooth, and the hair on his chest was dark and tapered into a V that disappeared below the towel hugging his flat stomach.

When he padded back to his side of the bed, she stealthily turned her head so she could continue admiring his lithe male body. He turned his back and dropped the towel. Hastily she shut her eyes again but not before she'd caught a glimpse of his trim buttocks and thighs. Now her heart and thoughts raced with panic. Did his disdain for any kind of covering mean he was contemplating rape? She knew there were men who found mutual dislike a turn-on. Was he one of those? The bed creaked as he lay down and she held her breath—half in dread and half because of some other, unfamiliar emotion. Then he turned his back on her and settled himself for sleep. Rape didn't appear to be on his mind, and within minutes he was breathing deeply and regularly.

Unlike Leo, sleep refused to come to Lucinda. He might snore away as if he was couched on a bed of swan's down, but this particular bed was the most uncomfortable she had ever lain in. Not only did the mattress seem to be stuffed with pebbles, it sagged and she had to cling to the edge with both hands to prevent herself from sliding to the middle. She clung grimly to her side of the bed, waking every time she dozed off, for then her hands relaxed and she started sliding toward Leo's warm, naked body.

Toward dawn she became so weary she gave up the struggle and rolled against him. She was cocooned in her blanket so she couldn't feel the texture of his skin, except for his shoulder, as smooth as marble against her cheek.

She woke alone in the center of the bed. Leo was nowhere to be seen. Hurriedly she groped for her glasses. Her watch said 5:45, and pale light splintered through the curtains. She could hear the call of gulls and the gentle lap of water. The storm seemed to have passed.

She leaped out of bed and started pulling on her clothes. Her jeans and heavy sweater were still damp and clung uncomfortably, but she wanted to be fully dressed by the time Leo came back. She was attempting to put some order to her hair, which was dull and unmanageable after being shampooed with the kitchen soap, when he came in. He was carrying a paper bag, which he waved under her nose.

"Dressed? Good! Then let's get a move on." He looked utterly refreshed, his blue eyes sparkling and alert, his movements brisk.

"Sleep well?" asked Lucinda bitterly, aware that her eyes were puffy and that her shoulders ached from fighting all night with that sagging mattress.

"Like a log!" He drew the curtains briskly to reveal a clear sky the color of pearls. "And you?"

"Very well," she lied, unwilling to admit she'd spent the night avoiding him.

"Don't moon around like a shell-shocked duck, then," he admonished. She gave up on her hair and put her comb back in her ditty bag, and slung it onto her shoulder. "I bought some bread and eggs and things. Thought it would save time to have breakfast on board." And with that he led the way out of the cabin.

It was a perfect morning, calm, with a light breeze that just ruffled the surface of the gently moving sea. Once they were under way, using both power and sail in order to make time, Lucinda went below and prepared their breakfast. He'd bought bacon as well as half a dozen eggs, a loaf of bread and a package of cheese. She cooked all the bacon and toasted several slices of bread. She was starving after their meager supper last night. The smell of the frying bacon was so delicious it took all her control not to wolf down her share as it cooked.

Leaning out of the hatch, she asked, "How do you like your eggs? Once over lightly, or sunny-side up?"

"Which is the one that's nice and runny?" The wind was ruffling his hair into steely curls that fell attractively over his forehead. Lucinda envied him his hair, particularly this morning when her own was such a mess.

"Sunny-side up."

"What a language! Sunny-side up for me then, please."

"Why don't you try learning some American?" she suggested frostily. "Improve yourself."

Back in the galley she put his share of the bacon and toast on a large plate with four of the eggs, and took it up to him.

"That smells wonderful." He took the plate from her and put on the automatic pilot. "You're going to bring yours up on deck, too, aren't you? You're not going to molder below?"

"I never molder," she informed him, "contrary to what you may believe."

"I don't believe I've thanked you for your help during the storm." He took the knife and fork she handed him. "You were a great help."

"What did you expect me to do? Fall apart at the seams?"

"Well, from the way Charles and Fran—"

"My family likes to tease," she broke in. "I'll make coffee for us later. Okay?"

"You're the cook," he said with a smile, but she didn't respond. She was fed up, and smiling was not on her morning's agenda.

She brought her plate on deck and seated herself at the far end of the stern and attacked her breakfast hungrily. Sea gulls hovered with beating wings, while *Yankee Doodle* pranced through the water like an elegant sea horse.

She made the coffee and took hers to the bow, leaning against the rail watching *Yankee Doodle*'s prow slice through the green water. She didn't want to talk to Leo. She didn't like him. All she wanted was to get home as soon as possible and forget him and this whole misadventure.

She spent the rest of the morning sweeping up rice grains and cereal, and putting things to rights below. When they were nearing the mouth of the river, she

prepared lunch—cheese sandwiches and a can of to-
mato soup from the cupboard, which she poured into
two wide-mouthed mugs and put on a tray.

She had just come up the companionway when Leo
changed course to negotiate the turn and the boat
changed its angle of heel. Lucinda, still holding on to
the tray, executed a sort of pas de deux across the
deck, wound up in front of him and tipped the tray
onto his lap. Leo bellowed as hot soup poured over
him.

"I'm sorry... I'm sorry," she cried.

"You shouldn't be allowed on a boat," he said
through clenched teeth. "You're a bloody menace."

"That's not what you said at breakfast." She
mopped ineffectually with a paper napkin. "You
should have warned me you were going to change
course."

"You knew where we were. Why didn't you use
your head? And stop dabbing at me, you're only
making it worse." The napkin was shredding and
sticking to his trousers in stained pink blobs.

Her eyes grew darker. "I'm only trying to help."

"Well, don't!" he snarled, taking hold of the tiller
and righting *Yankee Doodle*. "Sit down somewhere
out of the way and try not to do any more damage. I
have a plane to catch and I'd appreciate it if I could get
to the airport before you ruin the rest of my clothes."

"I have apologized," she said with dignity. Picking
up the sandwiches from the deck, she put them back
on the plate.

He looked scandalized. "Are you going to eat those?"

"Sure!" She brushed at them with a paper napkin. "The deck's clean." She passed the plate, but he shook his head. "Not for me, thank you."

"My land! Are all Englishmen so fussy?"

"Hardly fussy," he snapped. "Having been scalded on a sensitive part of my anatomy, I've lost my appetite."

She took a bite of sandwich and he gave her a look of loathing. "If you're going to stuff yourself, would you please do it somewhere else."

Tight-lipped, she picked up the tray and headed for the companionway. "Bad-tempered men tend to make me throw up, as a matter of fact," she said over her shoulder.

"Bad-tempered! It would take a saint to remain good-tempered with you around," he said.

"Well, no one could mistake you for one of those." She slammed the hatch shut.

In the galley she flung the rest of her sandwich into the garbage. She was glad she'd spilled soup on him. She should have dumped it on his head! She started noisily washing the mugs. She was sick of people putting her down. Sick of being the butt of jokes! She scrubbed at the saucepan as if it were Leo's head. She wished it were his head. She'd like to twist her fingers into that thick gray hair of his and pull and pull, till he fell off his damned high horse!

She stayed below, out of his way, until he called her to help him dock, then the only words he spoke were orders, given curtly and with no eye contact. She was still mad at him, and her temper seemed to lend her an agility she didn't normally possess. Her father would have been amazed.

When they'd tied up he went below to collect his things, and she started swabbing the deck. He returned carrying his leather jacket. It was now stiff as a board. She noticed soup stains on his slacks and his cream sweater as well. She had an insane desire to laugh, which she suppressed, and pushing her glasses firmly onto her retroussé nose, said, "I'll tell my father that you approve of *Yankee Doodle*, shall I?"

"Put that mop away," he said. "There's no time for that. Not if I'm to drive you home, and make it to the airport on time."

She returned to her mopping. "I want to clean up here. I'll get a lift home later... or walk. It's only a couple of miles."

"As you wish." He took a firmer grip on his zippered bag. "I'll say goodbye then."

She looked at him, her clear brown eyes neutral. She didn't let go of the mop and he didn't offer his hand.

"Goodbye," he said again, and leaped to shore. She watched him stride to his car, and when the engine caught she went back to her mopping without a second glance.

"Goodbye and good riddance," she muttered, savagely scrubbing at *Yankee Doodle*'s deck.

She opened all the hatches in order to thoroughly air the yacht, and then spent the rest of the afternoon relaxing with a magazine. The peace, once Leo was gone, was blissful; it must have been fatigue that made it seem flat.

The shadows were lengthening when she locked the hatches and started trudging in the direction of Small Port. A local farmer and his wife soon came by, and she gratefully accepted their offer of a lift, for she was now ready to drop in her tracks.

Charles's car was standing in the driveway, and her heart sank. She'd hoped that her father and stepmother wouldn't come home until she'd had a chance to shower and change out of her rumpled jeans. She'd have preferred to look a little less disreputable before dealing with them.

"Is that you, Cindy?" Fran called from the living room.

Fran and her father were sitting by the window, a frosty jug of martinis between them. "What's this I hear about you taking *Yankee Doodle* out overnight?" asked Charles. Lucinda found it depressingly typical that his first concern should be for his boat.

"We got caught in a storm—" she came a step into the room "—so we docked at the fishermen's wharf on Marshall's Island."

"Spent the night on board, did you? That must have been uncomfortable," said Charles with a mirthless chuckle.

"Was there anything to eat on *Yankee Doodle*?" Fran asked.

"We ate at a snack bar in the village." Lucinda took another step into the room. "And we didn't stay on board . . . because . . . because it was too damp."

"Too damp?" Her father put down his glass. "What do you mean, damp?"

"I...er...I left the hatches open by mistake." She added hastily, "But everything's fine. I dried her out this afternoon. She's shipshape again."

"Trust you to mess up," said Charles shortly.

"Poor Leo," cooed Fran. "I declare, he certainly got more than he bargained for."

"He wasn't the only one," observed Lucinda, going over to the martini jug. "Could I have one of these?"

"I didn't think you liked martinis," said Fran, surprised.

"I don't usually, but I'm tired and I feel the need for strong drink." She dropped an olive into her glass.

"Did you have to sit up all night in that...snack bar, was it?" inquired Fran.

"We spent the night at a motel and I didn't get any sleep. That's why I'm tired," Lucinda explained, sipping at her drink. It nearly made her gag, but the aftereffect was not unpleasant, so she took another, larger sip.

"A motel?" Fran said, her eyes opening wide. "I didn't know there was a motel on Marshall's Island."

"Chicken shed would be closer to the truth." Lucinda rashly topped up her drink. "They only have two units, and one of those is permanently out of commission."

"Where is Leo?" asked her father. "Did he bring you home?"

"No." She gulped more gin. "He's gone. Away. Very, very far away." She fished out her olive and chewed it thoughtfully. "He's got a...an appointment...in New York...or London. Someplace." The floor seemed to be moving slightly under her feet, and she was finding it difficult to focus. It felt most unpleasant, like being back on board *Yankee Doodle*. She put down her glass and carefully made for the door. "I think I'll just go and...and have a shower." She smiled muzzily.

"What you need is black coffee," her father said coldly.

Lucinda giggled. "Good idea. I'll get some... pronto!"

"What have you eaten today, Lucinda?" Em asked, when Lucinda came into the kitchen breathing gin.

"Breakfast...and...and one bite of a cheese sandwich...and an olive."

"And *that* came with one of Mr. Wainwright's martinis, I'll be bound," Em said. "Now you get on upstairs and I'll bring you something to eat."

Dutifully Lucinda left, pouring herself a cup of coffee to take with her. If this was what gin and vermouth did to one on an empty stomach, she didn't recommend it. She sobered up soon enough after her shower, though, but the mere *thought* of food made her feel sick, so, pulling on her dressing gown, she went downstairs again to stop Em preparing a meal.

The door to the living room was partly open, and her bedroom slippers made no noise on the parquet floor. As she passed on her way to the kitchen she heard Fran saying, "And I still think you should have asked outright. She's your daughter. You have a right to know if they slept together.''

"Come on, Fran!" her father replied. "Leo can have any woman he fancies. Cindy! Don't make me laugh."

Lucinda went cold. She knew her father didn't admire her, but she had never before heard him speak with such contempt. His careless tone was like a blunt knife tearing at her flesh, and she stood, unable to move, unable to stop listening. If she had moved she would have stumbled, and they would have found her at the door, and then she would have had to suffer Charles's anger as well as his scorn.

"I'm still not convinced," she heard Fran say. "Some men will sleep with anything if it's available."

"I'm sure Leo's not that desperate," her father said unkindly. "If it had been Trish...that's a different matter."

"If it had been Trish, she'd have come home with an engagement ring on her finger!"

Charles laughed.

Soundlessly Lucinda crept away from the door. She didn't want to hear any more. If she heard her father make one more thoughtless, cruel remark, she knew she would be unable to stop herself from going into the room and screaming at him. Screaming, screaming...spilling out all her years of hurt and frustration. And she didn't want to do that. She was shivering with fury. She had to regain her self-control.

"You look regular done in!" Em commented, when she went into the kitchen. "You shouldn't have come down again. There's some chicken soup and a bit of steak I can broil for you." But Lucinda would only accept the soup, and after a glance at her set face Em didn't insist.

Back in her room she was unable to sit still. The bowl of soup grew cold on the tray as she paced to and fro, to and fro, over the gleaming floor, filled with a savage and relentless anger.

Finally she climbed into bed and opened a book, although she knew it was unlikely she'd be able to concentrate enough to read. She heard the front door bang. Trish was home, and after a while there was a knock at Lucinda's door and her stepsister looked in.

"Hi! I saw your light still on." She leaned against the doorjamb, tall and lovely in her white track suit.

"How did the tournament go?" Lucinda asked, surprised that her voice sounded quite normal.

Trish made a face. "A bummer! We lost. I hear you had quite a time with *Yankee Doodle*. You've certainly given the parents something to talk about."

On no! thought Lucinda. *Not content with discussing my lack of sexual attraction between themselves, they've dragged Trish into it.*

"Mom seems to think you and Leo went to bed together," Trish went on. "Isn't that a hoot?"

Lucinda gritted her teeth. *Here we go again!* she thought. *Another vote of confidence from my nearest and dearest. Well, I've had enough!* She slammed her book onto the bedside table and yanked the sheets up to her chin.

"I always knew Fran was a woman who couldn't be fooled," she said, and clicked off the light.

CHAPTER FOUR

SHE HEARD TRISH GASP in the darkness. "You mean it's true?" Lucinda made a to-do of plumping up her pillows. "Is it true, Cindy?" Trish persisted. "Did you sleep with him?"

"Why don't you mind your own business?" suggested Lucinda.

"It is my business."

"I don't think so."

"Sure it is!" Trish's voice rose a decibel. "You stole him from me."

"I didn't know he was your property." Lying back on her pillows, she felt an alien feeling of power flood over her.

"I was working on it," Trish growled.

Lucinda said cheerfully, "Well, you left it a bit late. You could have bowed out of the squash tournament and gone sailing with him, shown him you really care."

"You bitch!" Trish said. "You devious little bitch."

"Calling me names isn't going to change anything," Lucinda said. "Anyway, he's gone now."

"I can't get over it," her stepsister moaned. "Going out of your way to seduce the guy I had my eye on."

"I didn't do any seducing," said Lucinda with a throaty chuckle, "and now will you please go away? I want to get to sleep. I'm tired."

"I'll bet you are!" Trish snapped. "I'll bet you're exhausted, you little slut!"

She slammed the door and clattered down the stairs, on her way, no doubt, to tell her mother about Lucinda's treachery. Lucinda could imagine Fran's astonishment. And what would her father say? He would hardly jump for joy to hear that his daughter had had a casual one-night affair. But he deserved a shaking up. If he were to believe this...this rumor, wasn't that a kind of rough justice?

She turned onto her side, blinking sleepily. Just the same...it was a lie and she'd have to tell the truth in the morning. Tonight, though, stringing Trish along had been fun. She wouldn't have missed her stepsister's baffled outrage for the world. Lucinda drifted into sleep, a smile on her lips.

Fran was waiting when she came down to breakfast. Her stepmother had been out for her morning jog and was drinking her first cup of coffee.

"Leave us alone, please," she said to Em, who was bustling about at the stove. "I want to talk to Miss Lucinda."

She always called the girls "Miss" to Em, to remind Em that she was a servant. This holdover from her Southern girlhood had always irritated Lucinda, for Em had been more of a mother to her than Fran ever had.

"Now, what's all this I hear?" Fran demanded when they were alone. "What's all this about you and Leo?"

"I told you that we spent the night together on Marshall's Island," replied Lucinda, pouring bran flakes into a bowl. "What do you want now? Details?"

"Trish tells me that you and Leo..." Fran trailed into silence.

"Leo and I...what?" Lucinda encouraged, pouring milk over her cereal.

Fran set her lips. "That you're his mistress!"

"You sound like a Victorian novel." Lucinda giggled. "All you need is a bustle and a bottle of smelling salts."

"I don't think it's Victorian to have certain values, Cindy. Frankly, I'm shocked. Very shocked indeed."

"You mean surprised, don't you, Fran?" Lucinda looked at her, her brown eyes steady. "Would you feel as shocked if it had been Trish who had spent the night with him?"

Her stepmother's eyes glinted. "Trish would not behave like a common tramp," she said.

"No. She would have come home wearing an engagement ring, wouldn't she?" Lucinda flashed, two bright spots of color on her pale cheeks.

Fran had the grace to look discomfited. "You heard that? Well, you know what they say, honey. Listeners never hear good of themselves."

"I'd have to wait a long time before I heard any good from Dad," Lucinda said bitterly, thrusting her bowl of cereal aside.

"What do you expect? He's very disappointed in you," Fran said, and added, "and in Leo, too."

"Come on, Fran! He's not disappointed in Leo. Surprised, maybe, that Leo was so desperate," said Lucinda hotly.

An ugly red crept up Fran's neck. "Now Cindy," she admonished, "you know your daddy doesn't always mean what he says."

"You mean that really he thinks I'm gorgeous, and he expected a man of the world like Leo Grosvenor to come along and seduce me?" Lucinda suggested, her delicate brows raised ironically.

"Well, if you insist on listening at doors," Fran complained. "Besides, honey, look at your track record. You're hardly the type to set the world on fire."

"Not the world perhaps," snapped her stepdaughter, "just the occasional man."

"I simply don't understand you, Cindy," said Fran getting angry. "You should be ashamed, not brazen like this."

"Well, I'm not ashamed," Lucinda replied with spirit. "And now I'm going to work."

Fran barred her way. "Cindy, I have to know the truth. I promise not to scold you anymore, but you must tell me. Did you, or did you not, share Leo Grosvenor's bed?"

"We shared a bed," said Lucinda evenly, and Fran drew in a sharp breath. "Now do stop behaving like a Tennessee Williams play. My life isn't ruined."

"He was just using you," Fran called after her when Lucinda went to the door. "It couldn't have been anything else, Cindy."

"I'm sure that's Dad's opinion, too," said Lucinda sharply, "and now let's drop it, Fran. Okay? It's over, and no harm done."

Fran followed her to her car, talking all the time. "I don't know about that. What if you're pregnant? Have you thought about that?" Her green eyes were sincerely troubled, and Lucinda patted her arm.

"I'm not, Fran. I can promise you that," she said, but her reassurance backfired.

"You mean you're on the pill?" Fran shrieked, pulling her arm away. "Cindy! Have you been carrying on behind our backs all this time?"

"If you'll believe that, you'll believe anything," said Lucinda, sighing heavily. "You promised to lay off, remember? Now let me go, Fran, or I'll be late."

As she drove off she was shaking almost as much as her little rattletrap car. Within the space of fifteen minutes she seemed to be sinking into a bog of half-truths. But what could she do about it? If she confessed the truth now, her family would never let her forget it and would mock her unmercifully for the rest of her days. And what about her father? He would despise her more than ever. She would not only be a dowdy embarrassment, but a liar as well. Another black mark against an already unsatisfactory daughter. There was nothing else to do but keep quiet until the whole thing had died a natural death.

One thing she could do, though, she decided as she drove across the causeway. She could change her image. She had always accepted her family's view of her, never even trying to make the best of herself. She would change that—starting now. She swung into the library parking lot with such verve that she almost sideswiped the head librarian's Chevy.

During the morning she phoned a hairdresser and made an appointment for late that afternoon. The salon she chose was one she'd heard her colleagues at the library mention. She didn't want to go to the sleek establishment Fran and her daughters patronized. It was a new Lucinda she was creating, not a pathetic copy of her stepsisters.

"You're looking on top of the world, Lucinda," said Olga, one of the girls she worked with. "You must have had a good vacation."

"It was...productive," Lucinda replied, sorting out a pile of books, "particularly this weekend."

"A great date, eh?" Olga, who was keen on men, nudged her.

Lucinda put a pile of nonfiction onto the trolley. "In a way."

"Well, whatever it was, it's sure perked you up."

That seemed to be true, she did feel good. It was as if being trapped with Leo on Marshall's Island had freed something in her. This odd, exultant mood lasted throughout the day, and when she came out of the hairdresser's that evening with her fine brown hair trimmed and lightly permed, she felt better than ever.

"You have very pretty hair," the hairdresser had told her. "It just needs a bit of help, that's all."

She stole a glance at herself in a store window on the way to the parking lot. Her hair did look pretty, floating around her face in loose bouncy curls.

"Cindy? I didn't recognize you," said a familiar voice, and she turned, nearly bumping into her brother-in-law.

"Hi, Del!" She ran her fingers through her shining tresses. "Like it?"

"Sensational! Makes you really look the part." She looked blank. "The femme fatale. Trish is over at our place now, bending Gina's ear. Yak, yak, yak! I left them to it."

Lucinda felt slightly sick. "Del, it isn't anything like Trish thinks. Really."

His good-natured face puckered into a grin. "You don't have to explain yourself to me, Cindy. I'm real pleased you had some fun for a change."

"But you don't understand—" Lucinda persisted.

"I don't have to, honey. It's not my business." She started to protest but he didn't listen. "Gotta rush, I'm bowling with the guys."

She called after him, "But Del!" He turned briefly.

"See you around, Cindy. *Love* the hair."

Frustrated, she watched his retreating back. The family seemed to have made up their minds. Well, did it really matter? Leo Grosvenor had gone forever so a little gossip wouldn't hurt him, and if the Wainwrights had decided their mousy little Lucinda had turned overnight into Circe, where was the harm? It might do the lot of them good.

"Your dad wants to see you," Em told her when Lucinda came in from garaging her jalopy. "He's in the living room." She looked at the girl critically. "The hair's a big improvement. Now get on in to your father while I warm up your supper. D'you want it here or in the dining room?"

"Here," said Lucinda, tucking her blouse, which had come adrift, neatly back into her skirt. It annoyed Charles to see her looking untidy.

"Don't let your dad spoil your appetite," said Em, with an old-fashioned look.

"I won't." But she already had that familiar sinking feeling. "Heat up the coffee, love, we'll both have a cup when I'm through."

Charles was standing by the fireplace. Experience had taught her that when he conducted interviews with her while standing she was in for a rough time, and her mouth grew dry.

He motioned her to a chair and then asked her if what she'd told Fran that morning was the case. "Fran says you and Leo slept in the same bed," he stated disbelievingly.

If he hadn't seemed so skeptical, Lucinda would have told him the truth there and then, but his air of incredulity acted like salt on the wound he'd inflicted the night before, and she tilted her small chin defiantly. "It's quite true."

He smoothed back his thinning hair. "I don't know what to say to you, Cindy."

"I wasn't expecting congratulations."

"Don't get smart. You've cheapened yourself. What must Leo think of you, throwing yourself at him like that?"

Stung, she protested. "I did not throw myself."

"You must have," said Charles bitterly. "He has never shown the slightest interest in you before."

"How do you know?" She blinked back angry tears. "Just because *you* think I'm a pathetic mess doesn't mean everyone feels the same."

"I don't think you're pathetic," blustered her father.

"Just a mess?"

"We're not discussing your appearance. We're discussing your behavior. And what about Trish? She's very upset."

"She's only upset because she thinks she's lost the chance of a manor house," explained his daughter. "She doesn't love Leo."

"Do you?"

"No," she admitted, "I don't."

"Just as well, because it's unlikely he'd feel the same."

She bit her lip so hard she was surprised it didn't bleed. "I know your opinion of me, Dad. I heard you and Fran discussing me last night."

"What do you expect, sneaking around behind doors?" he snapped guiltily. "I never questioned your moral code before. Seems I should have."

"I am twenty-two," she pointed out. "Isn't this heavy father act rather out-of-date?"

"Not if it stops you behaving like a trollop," he shot back.

She decided it was time to fight dirty. "If you feel so strongly perhaps you'd rather not live under my roof."

He turned a muted shade of purple. "And just how would you maintain this place without my money behind you?"

"I don't know. Take in boarders, maybe. I'd find a way."

"Now don't be silly, Cindy," he said, making an effort to control himself. "We're both too hot under the collar to discuss this rationally. I only brought it up because I'm concerned about you."

"That's a change," said Lucinda, under her breath.

"You're an inexperienced girl, and Leo Grosvenor... well, he's been around. I wouldn't want you to get hurt."

"I'm not and I won't be," she said crisply. She rose to her feet. "If that's all, I'd like to go now. My supper's getting cold."

"What's goin' on?" Em asked, when she and Lucinda were sitting at the kitchen table together over coffee. "Mrs. W.'s been like a bear with a sore head all day."

"They think I spent the night with Leo."

"Well, you did."

"They think we became lovers."

Em stirred another spoonful of sugar into her coffee. "Did you?"

"No!" Lucinda shouted. "We can't stand each other!"

"No need to bust my eardrums," Em complained.

"I'm sorry." She put her head in her hands. "Things seem to have gone out of control. This... rumor... started because Trish misunderstood something I said, and I let her because I was mad. I meant to put it right this morning, but then Fran started and I got mad all over again, and now everybody seems to think Leo and I are lovers. I met Del and he said Trish was telling Gina."

"What were you mad about?" Em asked.

"Something I heard Dad say... about me." Her voice broke and she took a hasty sip of coffee.

"If I know Gina," said Em, "this'll be all over town by morning."

Lucinda nodded in gloomy agreement. "I suppose it doesn't really matter. I mean, it's only my reputation that's affected."

"It's not only *your* reputation," Em reminded her sharply. "What about Mr. Grosvenor?"

"He lives in England for heaven's sake." Lucinda jerked her cup so hard her coffee slopped onto the table. "He won't know."

"Mind what you're doing!" Em got a dishcloth to mop up the mess. "That doesn't change the fact that it's a lie, does it?"

Lucinda took the cloth. "Let me do that. I haven't lied, Em. I just haven't explained, that's all."

Em looked at her severely. "Haven't you ever heard of the sin of omission?"

"Well, it's too late now," said Lucinda stubbornly. "Don't you see, Em? If they learn the truth now, Fran and the girls will never stop laughing, and as for Dad—" She bit her lip and flung the dishcloth in the direction of the sink, where it fell with a plop to the floor.

Em picked it up and put it on the counter before saying, "It's your business, Lucinda, but no good ever came from rumors. Just bear that in mind."

But for once Em seemed to be wrong. As the week passed, Lucinda noticed a change in her family's attitude. Trish might still be hostile, but there was a hint of wariness about her, and she treated Lucinda with a little more caution. Charles seemed so shaken by the suggestion that they move out of Cliff Top that he stopped nagging her every time she tripped, or dropped something.

Lucinda's mood of energetic self-improvement continued. She cleared out her closets and ruthlessly discarded any garment she felt unhappy with. The Nearly New Shop in town had never had such a bonanza. The few things that remained had the enormous shoulder pads ripped out and the skirts shortened.

For the first time in her life she refused to go sailing with the family on the weekend. "I have a date," she'd told her startled father, not adding that her date was with Olga, and that the two of them planned a shopping spree.

They started their afternoon by getting Lucinda fitted for contact lenses, before scouring the boutiques along the town's restored nineteenth-century Front Street for bargains.

When Lucinda's little car was crammed with boxes and bags, the girls sat on one of the old-fashioned benches that dotted the brick sidewalk and ate ice cream cones.

"Want to come to the theater tonight?" Olga asked her between licks. "I'm going with the crowd I hang out with. I can easily get you a ticket. I know the people who run the theater."

Lucinda accepted eagerly. Life really did seem to be taking a turn for the better.

She dashed home to shower and change into one of her new dresses, a shell-pink chiffon that molded her full young breasts and swirled around her hips. After hurrying downstairs, clinging tightly to the banisters for she was wearing new shoes and didn't want to do one of her famous tumbling acts, she poked her head around the kitchen door.

"I won't be in for supper, Em," she said breathlessly. "I'm going out."

"Let's have a look at you," Em demanded. She examined the soft-hued dress, as delicate as moonlight, and the earrings, two trembling slivers of metal that hung on either side of Lucinda's heart-shaped face. "Not bad," she pronounced finally. "Pity it takes a lie to get you to make yourself over."

Lucinda said sharply, "Don't nag, Em."

But Em insisted stolidly, "I'm not naggin'...just tellin'."

"Well, don't. And don't wait up for me, either. I may be late." She grinned. "At least I hope so." Going over to the old woman, she gave her a hug. "Please don't be cross, Em. I've had such a great day, you mustn't be cross."

Em's eyes were gentle, but she said tartly. "Get going then, or you'll make me miss my television."

"You and your blood and violence," Lucinda teased. "See you in the morning."

On her way into town she passed *Yankee Doodle*'s berth. She could see the top of her mast across the meadow, bobbing gently on the evening tide. This time last week she and Leo had been battling the storm. What a long time ago that seemed. She found herself wishing he could see her now in her new dress, her hair a cloud of soft brown curls. The girl he had known was either a salt-stained wreck or a parody of high fashion.

What was the matter with her? She put her foot down on the accelerator, and the rackety little car shot forward. The last person she wanted to see was Leo Grosvenor. The very idea that he might learn of the gossip about them made her blood run cold. Let him stay in his manor house in Sussex, or Essex, or wherever it was. Anywhere, so long as he was a long, long way from Maine.

Olga's friends were a pleasantly mixed group, some of them students at nearby Bowdoin College, the others working in town. They were all friendly to Lucinda, particularly one young man named Ed, and her initial shyness soon disappeared. After the play they went to a popular late-night restaurant for a bite to eat.

"We can dance there," Ed said. "You like to dance?"

"I'm not very good at it," she confessed, remembering Trish's howls of derision whenever she got on a dance floor.

"You'll be fine," he assured her.

And sure enough she was. In any case the floor was so tiny and so crowded that nobody could see what anyone else was doing, and you didn't have to be an expert.

When their food was served, Lucinda was seated next to Olga. "Having fun?" her friend asked, licking mayonnaise off her fingers. Her mouth full, Lucinda nodded. "Saw you on the floor with Ed," Olga whispered. "He's nice, eh?"

"Very nice," Lucinda agreed.

"He's gone on you," confided Olga, daintily nibbling a french fry.

"My God! It *is* you!" exclaimed a high-pitched voice, and Lucinda felt herself go cold. Her stepsisters' voices were not their most attractive features, and she would have recognized Gina's strident tones anywhere. "Del said it was," Gina continued, an expression of irritated bewilderment on her face. "What have you done to your hair?"

"It's called a perm," said Lucinda, swallowing with difficulty. "And if it comes to that, what are you doing here? Why aren't you out white-water canoeing or something?''

"We just dropped by for a sandwich."

Gina examined her stepsister intently. Under this scrutiny Lucinda's fingers grew awkward and she spilled a drop of ketchup onto her dress. "Damn!" she exploded.

Gina smiled. "You really ought to wear foul-weather gear when you eat, Cindy."

"Here!" Olga dipped a paper napkin into a glass of water. "This should fix it."

"Why aren't you sailing with Mom and Dad?" Gina demanded.

"I had other plans."

"Has she been stealing anybody else's man?" Gina asked Olga sweetly. "It's a new habit of hers."

Lucinda's cheeks grew hot, but Olga replied, "I don't know what you're talking about. You must have a screw loose."

"Just ask her what she was up to on Marhsall's Island if you don't believe me," Gina replied. She frowned as she glanced over to a far table where Del was waving his arms like a semaphore gone mad. "I'd better be off. As for your perm, Cindy, it's too tight. It's bound to frizz."

"What a bitch!" said Olga when Gina had left them.

"She's mad at me at the moment," Lucinda, explained, automatically defending her stepsister.

"She's always mad," Olga insisted. "My sister hated her in school." Olga had an older sister who had been in the same class as the twins. "Just the same," she went on, "what did happen on Marshall's Island? I can't help being nosy."

"I got stranded there in the storm last Saturday night." Lucinda screwed up the paper napkin and put it with the other debris on her plate. She could feel Olga's blue eyes on her, alight with curiosity. "I was with a man at the time."

"Somebody else's man?"

"Just a . . . a friend of the family."

"How old a friend?" asked Olga, far too interested now to let the subject drop. "Was he in his dotage?"

"He's thirty-three, if you must know." Lucinda was now too annoyed for caution. She could have cheerfully murdered her stepsister. By mentioning the events of last weekend she had somehow revived the memory of Leo. Now Lucinda half expected him to walk into the restaurant, tall and rangy, his astonishing hair falling untidily over his forehead, some cutting witticism on his lips. Without thinking, she said, "Mind you, he looks older because of his gray hair."

Olga gave a little shriek. "You don't mean that dreamy English guy at the shipbuilding works?" Lucinda didn't answer but her sudden color gave her away. "Oh wow! You lucky thing. No wonder Gina's mad. She's jealous! I'm jealous myself! He's a hunk!"

"Don't be so dumb!" she snapped crossly. "Anyway he's not that gorgeous, and he has the personality of a bad-tempered grizzly."

Her friend was not about to be put off. "Now, Lucinda, you can play it as cool as you like, but you said yourself that the weekend was...what was it? Productive!" She gave a crow of laughter. "Now I know what you mean. But why aren't you with him tonight?"

"He's gone home to England," said Lucinda shortly.

"Oh, poor Lucinda! Never mind, honey. He'll be back."

Lucinda replied swiftly, "He won't, and that's just fine with me."

Olga gave her hand a squeeze. "That's right, Lucinda. Put a brave face on it."

"I'm not doing any such thing!" Lucinda protested. But Olga was caught up in her own drama and wasn't listening. "It always helps to put on a brave face when your heart is broken," she informed Lucinda solemnly.

"My heart isn't broken," Lucinda squealed.

Olga looked at her owlishly and said, "It's all right. I understand."

The waitress brought their dessert and the rest of the party drifted back to the table, but this time Lucinda found it impossible to join in the fun. She knew that Olga would soon tell all her friends about Lucinda's "love affair." Not that she was malicious, but she simply couldn't resist intrigue, and the more Lucinda protested, the more convinced Olga would be that she was merely putting on a brave act.

Well, thought Lucinda, I'll just have to grin and bear it. Soon another piece of gossip would come along, and Lucinda's "affair" with the Englishman would be forgotten.

The next day Olga phoned to invite her to a picnic on Popham Beach with the same group, and Lucinda accepted. Surely the best way to squash rumors of unhappiness was to be seen often, and in excellent spirits.

She had a great time. They had scuba equipment, and Olga went off with the others to search for clams, while Lucinda went for a swim. She was a good swimmer, although her father complained because she wasn't speedy. "Cindy will never make the Olympic team!" was a regular dig.

After her swim she changed into shorts—new ones, bright blue and very short to make her legs look longer—pulled on a yellow T-shirt and went for a walk along the beach. She spent more time on her walk than she intended because she stopped to watch the terns feed in the receding tide. She arrived back as everyone was busy organizing the clambake. She noticed one or two of the girls looking at her sympathetically and guessed that they thought she had wandered off alone because she wanted to brood over her departed lover, so she made a concerted effort to be the life of the party, and flirted mildly with Ed, who seemed delighted by the sudden attention.

The sun was setting when they packed up the picnic things. Ed, who was hovering around her while she sorted out bottles in the cooler, asked her to finish the evening by going with him for a drink.

They drove in Lucinda's car to a little bar near the old fort at Popham. She knew every stone there. It was a refuge she often escaped to when things got tough at home. She used to try to recreate the fort in her imagination, the way it must have looked in 1861 when the semicircular granite walls had first been erected and soldiers in bright uniforms had bustled about the place. The central court was now a grassy enclosure, and picnic tables stood next to the marks of old gun emplacements, but sometimes, at twilight, she imagined she could hear ghostly voices mingling with the sound of the water slapping against the stones.

"Nice view," said her companion.

She looked out at Wood Island, a dark, thickly wooded shape rising out of a copper-tinted sea. "Beautiful."

"I didn't mean the island," said Ed gallantly. "You're a very pretty girl, Lucinda. You know?"

She pushed back her tangled curls, which contrary to Gina's prediction had not frizzed. She hoped Ed wasn't going to get serious about her. While it would be nice to have a male companion, she had no desire to become serious.

"I like you, Ed," she said, having decided to nip any romantic notions he might have in the bud, "but . . ."

"It's okay," he said before she had a chance to finish her sentence. "I know you're still carrying a torch for that English guy. Olga told me about it. But he's gone, and I'm here.'' He smiled, showing an attractive gap between his teeth. ''And I really do like you.''

It was nice, looking attractive, but it sure complicated things. ''I like you too, Ed,'' she said.

''That's great!''

''But the operative word is *like*,'' she repeated firmly. ''If we're going to be friends—''

''Friendship can grow into something more,'' he insisted.

She settled her glasses more firmly on her tip-tilted nose. ''It can, but it won't.''

He looked at her lugubriously. ''You've really got it bad, eh?''

Exasperated she snapped, ''No, I haven't! He's an arrogant son of a bitch, if you must know.''

But Ed just looked knowing and said, ''Women often fall for guys like that.''

''Look, Ed,'' she stated as patiently as she could, ''it's not what you think. I can't explain it now—''

''You don't have to,'' he told her. ''I can see how much you care for him. We'll just be friends...until you get him out of your system.''

Ed was scrupulous about keeping his distance after that. Over the next weeks she saw a lot of him, both with Olga's crowd of friends and alone, and if he seemed about to make a pass she had only to look sad and sigh deeply and he'd get the message. He kissed her sometimes, but they were very brotherly kisses. Actually Lucinda would have enjoyed something a little less brotherly, but she had created the role of a lovelorn heroine for herself and she was stuck with it.

By the time July had ripened into August, Ed's devotion was beginning to get on her nerves. She was also feeling guilty, for the ridiculous rumor hadn't died down yet. At home she had inadvertently fueled it herself. She had written away to a bookstore in England to inquire about a nineteenth-century novel she wanted, and when the reply arrived, Fran's sharp eyes had spotted the British stamp.

"So you do hear from Leo," she'd said. When Lucinda started to protest, she'd held up her hand majestically and refused to listen. "It's really none of my business, honey. I just pray he doesn't hurt you."

As for Charles, he seemed to have decided to ignore anything to do with his daughter, which was a lot easier for her to take than his previous peevish criticisms.

In spite of these minor problems, Lucinda had a good summer. The weather was particularly good this year, and she managed to swim at least once a day. For the first time in her life her white skin became faintly tanned to a luscious peach hue. She knew she had never looked better, and this lent a bounce to her stride, and a tilt to her small round chin.

One Saturday morning she came home after her children's reading group to find an unfamiliar car parked in the driveway. She put her own little auto in the garage and collected her purse and briefcase. She was wearing a new lilac cotton sundress, which left her golden shoulders bare. She'd fastened her hair high on her head with a white clip for the sake of coolness, and some curly tendrils had come free and hung on her slender neck. Her eyes, no longer hidden behind glasses now that she had contacts, looked enormous, and soft as dark brown velvet.

She came in through the front door, for the back porch had been freshly painted. No sooner had the door closed behind her than, as if on cue, Em appeared from the kitchen. Her lips were pursed grimly, a sure sign that she was agitated. "Lucinda! Here a minute," she whispered, signaling frantically.

"What's up?" Em was not usually dramatic.

Before the old housekeeper had a chance to reply, Fran appeared in the living room doorway. "Home at last," she said. "We've been waiting for you."

"What *is* going on?" laughed Lucinda. "I feel as if I'm in the middle of a French farce with all these doors opening."

"Come on in." Fran smiled benignly. "I've got a surprise for you."

The windows of the living room faced south. Sunshine glittered on the white walls and danced off the brass table lamps, so that for a moment Lucinda was too dazzled to recognize the male figure standing silhouetted against the windows. All she registered was the breadth of his shoulders and the lean height of him. Then her eyes adjusted to the glare and she saw his shock of gray hair. As if through a zoom lens zeroing in on a face in a crowd, Leo Grosvenor's features came into her focus.

"Oh, no!" she croaked, horrified.

"Surprise, Surprise!" Leo said. His eyes were blazing but he sounded as smooth as any lover. "I've come back," he said. "I've come back to you, Lucinda."

CHAPTER FIVE

"NO GIRLISH CRY OF JOY?" inquired Leo, coming over to her. Then he looked at her, glowing golden in her pretty dress, and said, "Lucinda?" She didn't answer, and he swept her into his arms and kissed her expertly. She was so surprised she didn't try to fight him off.

"Now, now, you two!" Fran reproved coyly. "Plenty of time for that when you're alone."

"We've missed each other," said Leo, taking a firmer grip on Lucinda, who was attempting to squirm out of his embrace.

"Well, she hasn't exactly been eating her heart out in your absence," Fran volunteered. "Her social calendar's been very, very busy."

"I wouldn't expect her to live like a nun," remarked Leo.

Fran said bitterly, "Not much chance of that!"

Lucinda found her voice again. "What are you doing here?" she quavered.

"Took you by surprise, did I?" He gave her a cold, hard smile. "Well, that's only fair. You've given me a couple of surprises just lately."

"Didn't you tell Cindy you were coming?" Fran asked him. She turned to her stepdaughter. "Didn't he tell you in his letters?"

"Letters?" said Leo, his brows rising.

"Well, I only did see one," Fran confessed, "and you never phoned. Or if you did, Cindy never told us about it."

"Didn't she? I'm amazed," he said dryly.

Lucinda finally managed to pull herself out of his arms. "Fran, I want to be alone with Leo. *Please!*" she implored, when Fran showed no signs of moving.

"Well...sure...if I'm in the way."

"You are," said Lucinda bluntly.

"I can understand that you want to be alone with him," Fran said, "but aren't you being a little over-eager, honey? I mean...can't it wait?"

"No!" snapped Lucinda, "it can't."

Fran gave a disconcerted giggle. "You certainly are frank." She said to Leo, "I don't know what you've done to our little girl, but she sure has changed."

"I don't know what I've done, either."

"Fran, I must talk to Leo," cried Lucinda, desperate.

"Be still, Cindy!" Fran turned to their unexpected guest. "You're sure I can't persuade you to stay for lunch? Just a scratch meal, mind, but—" she smiled at him archly "—you're practically one of the family. Although I must confess I had hoped things would have worked out...differently. We just couldn't believe it at first. You and Cindy!"

"It is difficult to believe," Leo said.

Lucinda turned scarlet. "Fran," she croaked, "please..."

Leo put a heavy hand on her shoulder. It felt like the hand of doom. "Lucinda and I do have things to discuss, Fran. I'll take her out to lunch, all right?"

"You don't have to ask my permission," said Fran with an air of injured dignity, as with a smile Leo opened the door for her. She stopped on the threshold. "It's too bad her daddy's out right now. I know he'll want to talk to you."

"I'm going to be around for a while," Leo said, much to Lucinda's dismay.

After firmly closing the door, he leaned against it, looking down at her. She had the impression that either he'd grown taller or she'd shrunk. "Well!" he said finally. "What have you got to say for yourself?"

"I can explain," she promised.

"I'll bet you can." His chin, which seemed stronger than she remembered, jutted uncompromisingly. "I underestimated you, Lucinda. I seem to remember that you work in a library. I didn't realize that you created the fiction for it, too."

She twisted her fingers. "I know it looks that way—"

"Damn right it does!" He moved into the room and she backed away from him, like an animal at bay. "For your information, the office staff at the works are convinced that the principal reason I've returned here is not because of a new contract, but because I want to revive my steamy affair with you."

She felt the color rise from the soles of her feet to the crown of her head. "How...how long have you been in Small Port?" she whispered.

"Three days, and during that time I've learned some astonishing things. I happen to be staying at a guest house this time, not a hotel. My landlady is a very moral lady, and it didn't take her long to let me know that she thought I should...'make an honest woman of you' was the phrase she used." His lips curled. "As if one could turn a liar into an honest woman by slipping a ring on her finger!"

"I never lied," said Lucinda, who was now backed into a corner. "I mean I never actually *said* we were lovers."

He leaned his arm against the wall, blocking any possible escape. "You just let people assume it, eh? Let the scandal proliferate like a bunch of damn rabbits."

"I honestly didn't know it would." She was getting a crick in her neck from looking up at him. "It got out of hand."

He gave an ironic snort. "So it would appear. What I don't understand is why you didn't put your family into the picture. Why not squash the rumor at home base?"

"I couldn't." Her face crumpled. "It started here."

"All the more reason."

She found her courage again. "You didn't exactly help to squash the rumor. Kissing me like that!"

That seemed to take a little of the wind out of his sails. "I don't know why I did that," he said, dropping his arm. "It must have been the surprise."

"Do you always kiss women when you're surprised?"

"I didn't recognize you when you first came in," he said. "You completely bowled me over."

"I've only had my hair permed." She moved over to the sofa and sat down, not sure her legs would hold her much longer. "It's no big deal."

He sat in an armchair across from her. "It's more than that. You've changed inside, too... your whole demeanor... There's a spark in you now that was missing before."

"I've been feeling good about myself lately," she confessed.

He asked thoughtfully, "Because your family believed we'd had an affair?"

She nodded. "I suppose so. It's hard to explain... and I guess it's not exactly admirable... but because they believed that an outsider...someone with an air of glamour—" He made a face, but she insisted, "you do have an air of glamour, at least they've always thought so. Because they believed you didn't find me a jerk, I stopped behaving like one." She sighed. "I'd better get used to feeling like one again."

He put the tips of his long fingers together, pressing them against his lips. "Not necessarily," he said.

"Well I am a jerk, aren't I?" she burst out. "When people...when my family...find out the truth, they're really going to have something to talk about!"

"I think there's a way you might come out of it un-scathed." She looked at him uncomprehendingly and he went on. "For the next month or so we could act out the lie. We could pretend to be in love."

Thunderstruck she stared at him. "You...you mean...?"

"Go on pretending that I'm your lover. Yes."

"You must be crazy!" she squeaked.

"Don't panic. Rape isn't my style."

"And how long is this supposed to go on?" she asked, her voice as thin as wire.

"A couple of months should do it. I have to go back to England in October for a bit. By that time you can let it be known that our affair has cooled and we've decided to call it a day."

"Why the act at all?" she said in a more reason-able tone. "Why don't you just tell everybody the truth and be done with it?"

"That was my original plan," he said, "but I've had time to think. I'm not a vengeful man. Besides, I could look very shabby. It comes down finally to my word against yours, and I'm the stranger here; there's no guarantee I'd be believed. I might be viewed as a cad who refuses to admit his share of responsibility. I don't fancy playing that role, thank you very much."

"But why?" she demanded. "Why would you go along with such a crazy scheme? I can't believe it's because you like me—"

He broke in. "I don't know you. I'm just begin-ning to realize that."

"And you're going to act this . . . this lie . . . just to get to know me better?" She stared at him, her brown eyes wide. "I find that hard to believe."

He agreed. "Oh, I want something in return, of course."

"Of course!"

"I'm going to be very busy at the office, and I have to find a house."

Oh God! He's going to settle here.

"A house!" she gasped.

"And then I have to furnish it."

"Are you settling here permanently then?" she whispered, regarding him with frank dismay.

"More or less. I shall spend six months here, six months in England. I need a base in both countries."

It was as if a fog had rolled in off the sea and covered the sun. She could hardly find her voice to ask, "What exactly is it you want me to do?"

"Help me get organized," he told her. "Help me find a house, fix it up, that sort of thing."

"I do have a job, you know." She glared at him. "Or do you expect me to give that up?"

"Don't be silly," he reproved mildly. "It's only your spare time I want." He touched her cheek with his long finger. "I think you owe me a favor, Lucinda."

"You're being very kind," she muttered. If she hadn't been so rattled she would have added, and not a bit in character.

"That's settled then. Now, let's get out of here before Fran misunderstands the long silence and accuses us of making love on the sofa. Although . . . why not?'' He rumpled the cushions. "Let's give her something to talk about. Don't you dare touch them," he growled when she went to straighten them. Reluctantly she obeyed.

They viewed three houses that afternoon, stopping on the way to buy sandwiches to eat in the car. One of the houses had imposing marble benches on either side of the front door and fluted columns ornamented with carved pineapples. "Too fancy," Leo declared. The second house was a little frame affair, with peeling white paint and a charming run-to-seed garden. "Too small," said Leo. The third, a split-level bungalow on the banks of Kennebec River, he rejected because it was too modern.

"There's no pleasing you," complained Lucinda, who was hot and tired. "I don't think you know what you want."

"Oh yes, I do," he said. "I have a very clear picture in my mind's eye."

"Then we stand about as much chance of finding it as a snowball in hell," she grumbled.

They stopped at a small café in town for a cup of tea. Several tables had been placed on a wooden deck, and Leo chose one that was shaded by an old maple tree. After they ordered—tea for him and iced coffee and a square of gingerbread for her—they leaned back in their chairs watching the modest rush-hour traffic flow past.

"I know exactly what I'm looking for," said Leo, continuing the conversation. "A house that's fairly old, with a fine view of the sea and access to a beach.

A beach that's not used by too many people and where I can fish from the rocks. And I want trails to hike, and a sense of history brooding over me."

The waitress came with their order and he stirred the tea bag in the metal pot thoughtfully. "I'm sure there are places like that around here, only the estate agents don't seem to know about them."

Lucinda took a bite of gingerbread. "It's called real estate in these parts," she informed him, licking some crumbs from her delicately curved lips. "You want the old Bosco place."

He stopped pouring his tea. "The Bosco place?"

"Mmm!" She nodded and several curls fell over her forehead. She pushed them back. "Heron Cottage. It's been empty for years. I don't know if it's for sale, though."

"Why the hell didn't you tell me this before?" he demanded.

"You didn't tell me what you were looking for. I'm not psychic." She smiled, showing her dimple. "I haven't learned to read your mind yet."

"To think we've been pounding the pavement for nothing all this time," he said.

She murmured, "Sidewalk!"

"What?"

"Sidewalk, not pavement."

He pushed aside the teapot. "Where is this cottage?"

"In Small Port, about a mile from our house. It's built on a peninsula, so it has a view of the sea on two sides. And it has a beach."

"What are we waiting for?" he shouted. "It sounds perfect."

He leaped to his feet, but she stayed seated, nibbling her gingerbread. "There's no point getting excited. I don't know if it's for sale."

"There's every point," he urged, pulling her to her feet. "It's empty, you say?"

"It's been empty ever since old man Bosco died, but that doesn't mean you can buy it."

"It doesn't mean I can't. Let's go and take a look at it."

"But I haven't finished my coffee."

He passed a hand through his hair, so that it stood on end like a small boy's. "God give me strength! Finish it while I pay the bill and I'll see you at the car. And don't dawdle."

They didn't talk during the drive. Lucinda was wondering if she'd been unwise, mentioning Heron Cottage. It was one of her favorite places, and she wasn't sure she wanted it invaded by this imperious Englishman. If he did manage to purchase it, he probably wouldn't allow her to beachcomb there, and even if he did, the sense of isolation would be gone. She would be a trespasser on his property, aware of him with every step she took.

They turned onto the dirt road that ran along the coast, until they reached the rutted lane that led to the cottage. There was a chain looped across, bearing an ancient pockmarked sign: Private Road. "From here on we walk," she told him.

He switched off the engine, and the sound of the restless sea filled the silence. She ducked under the chain clumsily, turning her ankle and stumbling, and Leo's hand closed over her elbow, and stayed there. It felt oddly protective.

Silently they walked along the overgrown drive. It was late afternoon now, and the shadows stretched long under the sparse pine grove to their right. The scent of wild roses mingled with the tang of salt and resin. Gulls called in the cloudless sky, and the surf whispered unseen on the beach ahead. The track took a turn, climbed slightly, and suddenly Heron Cottage was standing to their left.

It wasn't a cottage at all, really, it was a large, rambling frame house, which had once been painted blue, but was now flaked and faded by time and weather. A sagging veranda clung drunkenly to the front. A picket fence—many of its posts missing, like a smile with missing teeth—enclosed a small garden, taken over now by wild roses and blueberry bushes. The garden gate lay flat on its face on an overgrown flagstone path.

"It's enchanting," said Leo, gazing raptly at his ruin.

Lucinda was not so enthusiastic. "It'll take a lot of money to fix it up," she cautioned.

He waved this aside. "Not so much. It's a solid house. Look at the roof, that's in good shape."

"I'll bet you the heating's not."

"Easily fixed," he declared. "And look at that view!"

She couldn't argue with that. Standing there look-ing at it felt like flying, with sea stretching to left and right, the coastline slashed with inlets and coves. The cliffs were covered in a thick carpet of juniper bushes, whose shiny dark green foliage was stabbed with vivid splashes of scarlet where Maine lilies grew. A dense wood of evergreens hovered near the back of the house.

He pointed to a barely visible track among the low bushes. "Is that the path to the beach?" She nodded. "Let's take a look."

On the beach the sand was coarse and yellow, un-like Indian Head. A low line of rocks hugged the cove, and a tumble of driftwood of every shape and size, from six-foot planks to splinters, gave evidence of the violence of the winter storms that battered this coast. A family of eider ducks bobbed up and down in the waves, and a cormorant plunged into the green water.

"I've found my American home," said Leo softly.

"That's all very well," Lucinda replied, "but you don't know if the place is for sale. You may not be able to buy it."

He set his chin obstinately. "I'll buy it if it's the last thing I do." And she sensed that he would succeed. Soon he would move in to Heron Cottage . . . and ruin it for her.

"It gets pretty wild here in the winter," she said, in a last-ditch effort to put him off.

"I like it wild. It matches my youth."

"Will you be giving up your house in England?"

"Certainly not! Cloisters has been in the family for years." He turned from staring at the horizon and asked, "Who do I see about buying this place?"

Slightly taken aback, she stammered, "I—I'm n-not sure."

"Come on, Lucinda!" he urged, "You've lived here all your life, you must know who owns it."

"When old Mr. Bosco died, there was some talk of a cousin in Vermont."

"When was that?"

"When was what?"

"When did this Bosco man depart this vale of tears?"

"About five years ago."

"Well, find out where this cousin can be reached, will you?" he said authoritatively. "I'd like to do something about the house this weekend."

"It won't be possible to find out tonight," she said, ruffled by his bossiness. "It's Saturday, and I have a date. In fact I have to get home now, or I'll be late."

She gave him a curt little nod and started up the track, but he caught her by her upper arm and swung her around to face him. "Oh, no you don't!" he said sharply. "No dates with other men for the next few weeks."

"What are you talking about?"

"I don't know how it is in America," he drawled, "but in England when a couple are having an affair they don't go on dates with other people."

She defied him. "I'm going dancing with a group of friends, and I don't intend to let you stop me."

"A group?" He let go of her arm. "Well, of course, that's different."

"Thank you!"

"I'll come, too."

She stared aghast. "You can't do that."

"Why not?" His eyes glittered like blue steel. "I'm house-trained."

"I mean…it's just…" She started to waffle. "We're going to a crummy little place. Nothing grand. Not the sort of thing you're used to."

"How do you know what I'm used to?"

"I can tell," she said with a snort. "You're the type who demands a fish knife when he opens a can of sardines."

He gave a bark of laughter. "I shall have to come now," he said, "if only to change my image."

"You haven't been invited."

"No problem!" He started leading her up the cliff path. "What could be more natural than to bring your lover along?"

"Maybe we shouldn't go at all," she said.

He stopped so suddenly she fell up against him, and he put his arm around her to steady her. It would have been nice to cling to him, but she righted herself and said, "There's no point in complicating things. The less people see us together, the better."

"Don't be daft, darling," he said. "If we're going to act the part of lovers we must be seen together. Particularly by your friends. They've heard about our passionate night on that godforsaken island."

Lucinda was about to protest, when she remembered Olga's whispered asides, and Ed's sympathetic backing off. Dear God, she prayed silently, don't let Olga say anything idiotic when she meets Leo.... But she had a sinking feeling that it would take more than prayers to repress the irrepressible Olga.

Leo dropped her off at the front door, and she went into the kitchen in a thoughtful frame of mind.

Em looked up from the evening paper. "There's cold ham and salad in the fridge," she sad, "if you want it."

Lucinda pulled a cold roast of beef out of the refrigerator and started carving, and Em put aside her newspaper. "Give me that knife, child, you'll cut off your hand if you carry on like that." She tidied up the roast that Lucinda had hacked, and then neatly cut another slice. Placing it on the plate, she asked, "Did Mr. Grosvenor give you a bad time?"

"No, he didn't. We've made a...sort of deal...but I can see problems ahead." She took a sliver of meat and popped it into her mouth.

"More problems? I should think you have plenty of those already."

"He's being very nice." She stirred the spoon around in the pottery mustard jar. "I've no idea why."

Em said crisply, "I always did say you had him figured wrong."

Lucinda helped herself to salad. "Let's not get carried away. He still throws his weight around. Hurls orders at me like a three-star general."

"I guess he's used to bein' the boss," Em remarked placidly. "What did he say about all the talk?"

Lucinda buttered a roll. "Not much. He figures if we pretend that . . . that Marshall's Island really happened, folks will forget about it."

Em's faded blue eyes opened wide. "When you say *pretend*, do you mean—"

Lucinda shook her head so violently some brown curls tumbled out of their clip. "No, no! It's just an act, Em."

"Seems strange to me," the old woman said. "What does he get out of it?"

"Help finding a house and furnishing it—stuff like that. Seems he's pretty busy right now and he needs a personal slave. I'm it!"

"Well!" Em looked slightly doubtful, "At least there won't be no scandal." She brightened. "Maybe you'll wind up gettin' to like him."

"Don't count on it," Lucinda replied with her mouth full. "And that's not all. I showed him Heron Cottage, and now he plans to buy it and live here in Small Port for part of each year. How does that grab you?"

Em received his news calmly. "The old Bosco place, eh! I guess Abigail Bosco will be right glad to get rid of it."

"Who?" asked Lucinda, fork poised.

"Abigail. She's Bosco's only livin' relative, so she inherited the cottage. But she lives in Vermont. I reckon she'll be glad to sell it."

Lucinda's great brown eyes gleamed. "Do you have her address?"

"Sure!" said Em. "We exchange Christmas cards."

"Em, you're wonderful!" she dropped her fork and went over to give her old friend a hug.

"I don't see what's so wonderful about havin' a friend's address," Em murmured.

"Take my word for it," Lucinda grinned happily. This would put a dent in Leo's imperiousness. He would never expect her to get the information this weekend. Well, she'd show him that she wasn't quite the little airhead he took her for. If he wanted things done instantly she'd prove she was the girl to do them. That should take a reef in his sail!

She got ready for the evening with a light heart. She wanted to look her best so she put on a full-skirted cotton dress, scooped low in the neck with a wide satin sash around the waist. It was more elaborate than this particular dance called for, but it made her feel like a million dollars. It was the color of butterscotch, dotted here and there with brown pansies that matched her velvety eyes.

She had time to wash her hair but not to set it, so it fell to her shoulders in a cascade of soft curls. She had been going to put it up again, but it looked so attractive loose that she decided to leave it alone. A tortoiseshell bracelet that had belonged to her mother and a generous splash of Anaïs Anaïs completed her toilet.

She was waiting on the front porch, Abigail Bosco's address and phone number in her purse, when Trish came up the drive, tennis racket in hand.

"What are you all dolled up for?" she asked. "A date with Leo? Mom tells me he's back in town." She sniffed at Lucinda critically. "You smell like a Chinese whorehouse."

"And when were you last in one of those?" parried Lucinda sweetly.

"I shouldn't think Leo would go for something so unsubtle."

"Maybe you don't know him very well," Lucinda suggested.

"Maybe not." Trish perched on the top step and crossed her long brown legs. "Frankly, I don't want to anymore. I've decided that as men go Leo runs pretty well to form."

Lucinda wondered if she'd also decided that manor houses in England and the cash it took to maintain them ran pretty well to form as well, but she contented herself by merely commenting that it was possible.

"I've just been playing tennis with a terrific guy," Trish informed her aggressively. "He makes Leo look like a wimp."

This was such an unlikely description that Lucinda giggled. "He must be quite something."

"He is," her stepsister said truculently. "He's dreamy."

Fortunately, at that moment Leo drove up. He got out of his car and Trish rose to her feet. "I don't know

whether to say 'hello stranger' or 'welcome back,'"
she remarked coldly.

He gave her a charming smile. "Why not both? You
look lovely, darling," he said, coming to Lucinda and
kissing her lightly on the cheek, "like a summer garden." Lucinda thought that he must be a very good
actor, for the admiration in his eyes looked quite gen-
uine. It would have fooled anybody. Anybody but her.

"We're late, Leo," she said. She wanted to get away
from Trish now, away from her hostility.

"Let's go then, angel." He tucked her hand under
his arm and nodded cheerfully at Trish.

"I'm not sure this is going to work," said Lucinda,
when they were speeding toward town.

"What do you mean?" he asked.

"I'm not sure I can fool people. Fool the family,"
she added. "I've always been a rotten actress."

He didn't take his eyes off the winding road ahead.
"You might try the odd endearment," he said. "It
wouldn't hurt."

"I don't think I'd be convincing," Lucinda said
uncertainly.

"No experience? Or are you just naturally reti-
cent?"

"I don't use endearments to people I don't like."

He slowed the car as they approached the city limits. "But you're supposed to like me. You're supposed to be in love with me, so the occasional
endearment would be in order."

She sighed. "I guess so. I'll work on it." She stared moodily at the large frame houses that bordered the road into town.

"You must have done a pretty good job in the past, when people asked you about our night on Marshall's Island."

"I never lied about that night," she protested. "I just didn't say anything."

"Well, don't say anything now if it bothers you so much." He gave her a quick smile. "Just cling and leave the endearments to me."

"You seem to be rather good at them," she observed. "I gather you've had experience."

He grinned. "I am thirty-three, angel. It would be unusual if I'd not had some love affairs."

"I suppose," she said, remembering his bad temper when he thought he might miss his date in New York.

"And I was engaged to be married once." She could hardly ask what happened, although she was dying to know, but he solved this by adding, "It was to a girl I've known all my life. We're still very close. Pam's keeping an eye on Cloisters for me while I'm away, as a matter of fact."

She gave a noncommittal grunt. It was nothing to her if this woman was dumb enough to let herself be used this way. Right now she had to get through the ordeal of introducing Leo to her friends, and no doubt watching him condescend to them. Come to think of it, that might not be such a bad thing. If he did put on his British patronizing act with them, they'd be understanding later on when she told them the affair was over. They might even feel happy for her.

But Leo charmed them. All except Ed, of course, who became very subdued as the evening wore on, for Leo was a tremendous hit. He made jokes, listened to the conversation with every sign of enjoyment, and he didn't draw attention to his superior financial position by insisting on paying for more than his share of the drinks. He'd even dressed right in navy slacks and blue-and-white-striped shirt, looking a great deal less ostentatious than Lucinda did in her flowery dress.

"I think your Leo's terrific!" Olga whispered when the men had gone off to get drinks for them. "No wonder you were so upset when he went away."

"I wasn't upset," Lucinda objected.

"Oh no?" Olga looked at her knowingly. "You can't fool me. I used to watch you, walking along the beach by yourself, eating your heart out."

"I like walking alone," protested Lucinda.

The younger girl smiled. "You don't have to put on a brave face any longer, honey. It's as clear as the nose on your face that he's mad about you."

Leo returned, carrying a tray of drinks, which he put down on the table. Olga said to him, "Lucinda's trying to kid me that she didn't miss you while you were in England."

"That's not true, is it, my darling?" he asked, looking at her sternly.

She fiddled with her fingers and finally mumbled, "Everybody seems to think I did, so it's no use denying it."

"My Lucinda tries to hide her feelings," he confided to Olga, "but it's all a fake. She seems quiet, but inside she's seething with passion."

Lucinda choked on a mouthful of ginger ale.

"Listen!" he commanded, "They're playing our song." He grabbed her hand. "Let's dance."

"We've already danced," she said shortly.

He clasped her firmly around her small waist. "This is a slow one, and I need to hold you close." He smiled at Olga, who was patently delighted by this demonstration of affection.

"Not the brightest thing in the world, telling that girl you didn't miss me," he muttered into Lucinda's ear when they were on the dance floor.

"Do you have to hold me so close?" she complained. "I can't breathe."

"We're supposed to be in the grip of hopeless passion," he said. "That means we dance as if we were stuck together with glue."

"I don't know about the grip of hopeless passion. The grip of King Kong would be more like it."

He leaned back for a moment to look into her eyes, "Haven't you ever been in love?"

"Not if being in love means you get crushed to death."

"Relax and enjoy it," he advised. "Besides, knowing your propensity for falling flat on your face, I should think you'd be grateful for the support."

"I don't fall down when I'm dancing," she protested. "Besides, I've improved."

"You certainly have," he agreed. "You've blossomed like one of the flowers on your dress."

"'A rag and a bone and a hank of hair'," she quoted, "I'm still the same inside."

"I disagree." He executed a difficult step and she followed without missing a beat. "You've lost that hangdog air. You were constantly apologizing for having been born."

She tilted her head back to look up at him. "You didn't help, always cutting me down to size."

"You got on my nerves. Frankly, I thought you were a perfectly dreadful girl."

She jerked away. "Gee, thanks!"

"I was mistaken," he soothed, pulling her back.

"You? Mistaken? Is that possible?"

"Of course. I'm not infallible."

"You could have fooled me."

He resumed their previous conversation. "You've become a very pretty girl. Mind you," he said, "I miss the glasses."

She stared at him. "You liked them?"

"Mmm!" His eyes twinkled. "They made you look like a vulnerable owl."

"An owl! Thanks a lot."

"I happen to like owls," he said, grinning. "I like the way their heads rotate."

She said, "My head is never going to rotate again if you don't loosen your hold." This is a kind of flirting, she thought. What am I thinking of!

The dance came to an end and he let her go. It felt lonely without his arms around her, which didn't make sense, considering she didn't like him.

She seemed unable to control her reactions tonight and that was nice in a way, but it was also unsettling, so she wasn't sorry when Leo suggested they leave. "We don't mean to break up the party." He smiled. "However, we have to make an early start tomorrow and find me a place to live."

"Oh boy! Does that mean you're going to move to Small Port?" asked one of the girls. "I'll bet you're happy about that, Lucinda."

"I'm delirious." That was stretching a point, but she didn't feel quite so unhappy about the prospect of having Leo as a neighbor. "Daddy will be waiting up," she lied. "We must go. I don't want him to worry."

"Heaven forbid!" drawled Leo, taking her arm.

"Goodbye, Lucinda," Ed called after them, "see you around... I guess." His eyes were as mournful as a spaniel's.

"I think that young man fancies you," Leo said, as they drove out of the parking lot.

"Much good it'll do me with you on the scene."

"You should thank me," he remarked airily. "I'm saving you a lot of misery. That boy's not right for you."

He'd gone too far, and she bristled, "You know nothing at all about me. Ed's a sweetie and I'm very fond of him."

"A sweetie is not what you need," he declared. "However, if you insist on throwing your life away, I can't stop you, so cheer up. When I'm out of your life for good, you can pursue him to your heart's content."

"Thanks for your permission," she growled, staring fixedly out the windshield.

They drove on in silence. It was a lovely night, soft and still, with a full moon that cast black velvet shadows under the trees. As they neared Small Port the smell of the sea blew in through the windows. She would have liked to be strolling along Indian Head Beach, barefoot on the cool wet sand . . . with Leo. . . . She must stop this mawkish train of thought. He might have been nice about things, but that was no reason to get sentimental over him. She must remember that she owed him a favor, not her heart.

When they drew up in front of her house, Leo didn't switch the engine off. "It's sweet of you to ask me, but I won't come in," he teased. "Give me your key and I'll open the door for you."

"We don't lock doors in Small Port." She clambered out of the car, catching the hem of her skirt in the door. Leaning across the passenger seat, Leo released it. "Don't be in such a rush, you'll tear that pretty dress." She could smell the clean scent of him, a mixture of soap, and after-shave and good fresh air.

When he walked with her to the front door, she smoothed her skirt around her thighs, as if the flimsy material were a protection, like armor. "Will you need me tomorrow?" she asked, attempting to sound businesslike.

"Please. We have to find out about Heron Cottage."

She remembered then about Abigail Bosco's address. "This is the person to contact," she said, fishing in her bag and triumphantly producing the piece of paper.

"That deserves an extra good-night kiss," he murmured, and before she had a chance to protest he had scooped her into his arms.

She was too surprised to resist. Too surprised to do more than wind her arms around him and respond. Her lips parted under his, like a flower opening in the warmth of the sun, and her breath caught in her throat while the world seemed to tilt on its axis.

Abruptly she came to her senses and tried to turn her head away, pushing at him ineffectually. He let her go almost at once.

"What's the matter, darling?"

"Please," she begged, "please don't complicate things." The moonlight was so bright she could see the color of his eyes, as blue and deep as water, and as unfathomable.

"You worry too much, Lucinda," he whispered, kissing the tip of her nose. "Sleep well."

In the darkened hall she leaned against the door, her legs trembling. This time when he kissed her she had wanted him to go on and on, for the touch of his mouth had released all kinds of delicious sensations that she had never felt before: a kind of languorous, quivering sensuality, which promised to grow into a passion such as she had never known; a passion that could destroy her—drown her....

Shivering with apprehension she crept up to the safety of her room.

CHAPTER SIX

LUCINDA HAD A SWIM before breakfast. Apart from a clutter of whitened clamshells, the beach was as smooth as a freshly made bed, for it was still too early for any people from town to have arrived to trample it. The water was calm, and she swam out quite far along a shaft of sunshine that made a shimmering path on the sea. Then she floated on her back, looking up into the cloudless blue vault of sky. The water was cool, but she figured that if she were going to burst into flames every time Leo kissed her, perhaps soaking in cold water would be beneficial.

A lean redheaded figure in a russet tracksuit came down to the beach and started jogging—Fran, doing the first of her daily workouts. Reluctantly Lucinda struck out for the shore. She didn't particularly want to see her stepmother right then, but the water was too cold to stay in any longer.

As she was wading out of the shallows Fran came up and started running on the spot. "You really should swim harder, Cindy," she said, panting. "It's pointless just paddling around like that."

Fran made this remark every time she saw Lucinda in the water, so Lucinda just smiled vaguely and proceeded to search short-sightedly in her beach bag for her glasses.

Fran stopped dancing up and down, and Lucinda, glasses now in place, noted that the early-morning sun wasn't kind to her stepmother. Her deeply tanned face had a leathery look, and the skin around her thin lips was funnelled with fine vertical lines. Lucinda felt a pang of sympathy. Charles set great store by his wife's youthful appearance.

They started back to the house, and Fran asked if Lucinda planned to see Leo.

"He'll be by after breakfast," said Lucinda, picking up her sandals and walking barefoot over the silvery sand.

"Good! Your daddy wants to talk to him."

Lucinda felt a tremor of unease. Was Charles—like Leo's landlady—about to demand that he make an honest woman of her? Not that Leo couldn't handle such a contingency. He seemed able to handle most things with aplomb, but it would be humiliating just the same.

They were approaching the house when Fran laid her hand on Lucinda's arm. "I hate to have to say this, honey, but I'd be neglecting my duty as your step-mama if I didn't."

Lucinda said quickly, "Please, Fran! There's no need."

Fran fiddled with the waistband of her sweat suit. "There's *every* need, honey," she said. "You think of yourself as a grown-up, but when it comes to men ... why, you're just a child! You've had no ex-

perience, Cindy. And Leo!'' She regarded her stepdaughter sympathetically. "Let's face it, you're just
not in his class.''

"Maybe I should date a different man each night till
I gain the experience I need,'' Lucinda suggested.

"Now don't get fresh,'' said Fran, piqued. "I'm
trying to help you.''

"Well, don't, Fran. I'm not going to stop seeing
Leo. I *can't*,'' she added, which was a fact, as long as
she was under an obligation to him.

"You seem regularly obsessed by him,'' observed
Fran moodily. "I declare, I don't recognize you these
days, Cindy. You're so smart-alecky…and look at you
now! Flaunting yourself in that bathing suit…
like…like…''

"Afraid I might shock the sea gulls?'' asked Lucinda, looking down the deserted beach. Until this
summer she had always worn a tank suit cut for racing, the kind her stepsisters wore, but while this style
might do wonders for Trish's and Gina's athletic bos-
oms, it squashed Lucinda's generous breasts into a
most unflattering shape. "I got tired of bulging out of
my tank suit,'' she said now, looking down at her new
cornflower-blue one-piece.

"Well, you just have to accept the fact that you've
got a difficult figure,'' said Fran. "Leo won't respect
you for flaunting it.''

Lucinda's self-confidence had improved a lot during the summer, but she was not totally immune to her
stepmother's tactlessness. She decided to end this lecture.

"I'm sure you mean well, Fran," she said, "and I promise you that nothing bad is going to happen to me. Now, let's give it a rest. Okay?"

She heard Fran call after her, "I warn you, Lucinda, if you cheapen yourself you'll regret it." But the only reply her stepmother got was the mewing of the gulls.

When Lucinda came down after her shower, she found Leo already in the dining room, drinking coffee with her father. Anxiously, she scanned their faces for signs of tension.

"Good morning, darling," said Leo, getting up to kiss her. She adroitly turned her head so that he was forced to kiss her on the cheek. "Such a shy little thing," he said to Charles dryly. "I can appreciate your concern." There was a smile on his lips, but his eyes were cold. "Your father's been explaining how much he *values* you, Lucinda," he said.

She looked at them warily. Leo was smiling grimly, but her father... What could have happened to give him this guilty look? Suddenly she felt as if she were walking a tightrope. Leo was angry; she recognized the signs. One wrong word from Charles, and he might get angry enough to tell her father the truth. She felt a knot form in her stomach as she said brightly, "Well, that's nice. Any coffee left?"

"I'm just trying to stop you making a fool of yourself," Charles blustered.

"Your father was telling me, Lucinda," Leo broke in, "that you're not used to having men admire you. A thing I find hard to believe."

Charles turned a dull red. "Just trying to protect the girl. I guess it's not necessary, but you know what fathers are."

Leo's expression was stony. "Indeed, yes."

"What do you say to a game of tennis this afternoon?" posed Charles, anxious to change the subject. "We can get some exercise."

"I'd enjoy a game of tennis," said Leo. He turned to Lucinda. "How about you?"

She took one of the rose-flowered cups and poured herself coffee, her hand shaking. "I don't play tennis."

"I tried to teach her," Charles huffed, "but it was impossible. She's totally uncoordinated."

Flushing, she stirred cream into her coffee. She remembered only too well those miserable hours on the court, with her father growing more exasperated at each hopeless swing of her racket. The humiliation the ten-year-old Lucinda had suffered under his scorn renewed. "I hate tennis," she said. "I'll find something else to do this afternoon."

"You can keep score," Leo suggested.

She didn't want to go near the tennis court if she could help it, and she said, "If I stayed home, I could try and get in touch with Mrs. Bosco for you."

"I've already been in touch with her," Leo informed her. "Fortunately, she's an early riser."

"And does she want to sell Heron Cottage? Did you get your own way as usual?"

"Of course. We're to go to Vermont sometime next week to discuss price."

"I do have a job, remember?" she snapped. Owing him a favor was one thing, being constantly at his beck and call was another.

"Of course you do," Leo smiled. "Don't worry, we'll fix something."

She went to help Em fix breakfast, and was careful to see that two of the fried eggs were served sunny-side up. "It's how Leo likes them," she told Em, who unaccountably smiled at her.

When she returned to the dining room, Fran and Trish were there, like her father, in sailing clothes. "We're taking *Yankee Doodle* out this morning," Trish said. "You'd better change out of that skirt, Cindy."

Lucinda put the platter of bacon and eggs in the center of the table. "I can't. I'm going to church."

Charles helped himself to eggs. "Rubbish, Cindy, there's a fresh breeze up. We'd better make use of it."

"I promised Em I'd take her," said Lucinda, popping bread into the toaster. "I promised," she repeated.

"I'm afraid you'll soon discover that Cindy is hopeless when it comes to getting off her bottom to do anything athletic," explained Charles, "and she's as stubborn as a mule. Neither reason nor common sense will budge her."

Lucinda knew that this was an oblique reference to her refusal to sell him Cliff Top, since he always used the same phrase when they had one of their long and fruitless arguments. She bit her lip, hoping silence would deflect him from his pet grievance.

"Next to owls, mules are my favorite animals," Leo murmured, shaking pepper over his eggs. She looked up at him quickly and he gave her the shadow of a wink. "I think I'll pass on the sailing and go with Lucinda."

Trish goggled at him. "What?"

"To church," he said. "You know this is my second breakfast this morning, and it's infinitely better than my first."

"You don't want to come to *church*!" protested Lucinda. Everybody from Small Port would be there. They'd see him with her and the rumors would fly worse than ever.

"Don't be so un-Christian, darling," He munched a piece of bacon. "I won't get to glory if you shut me out."

"You must be nuts, going to church on a great sailing day like this," said Trish.

"Leo's our guest, honey," her mother said reprovingly. "He can do what he likes."

"There'll be other days," he said. "I'm not dashing off to England this time." He regarded them all cheerfully. "I intend to become your neighbor."

"You're leaving England?" Fran gasped. "But . . . but what about your manor house?"

"What about it?" Leo asked. "It's been around for four hundred years, I don't think it will crumble to dust simply because I'm not in continuous residence." He took a bite of toast. "I'll be there six months of the year, and I've friends who will keep an eye on it in my absence."

"Did I hear you mention the old Bosco place?" asked Charles. "Thinking of settling there, are you?"

Leo nodded. "That's right."

"People around here say it's haunted," Trish told him, in the same tone that she might have informed him about cockroaches.

Leo put a spoonful of blueberry preserve onto his plate. "Cloisters is haunted, too. The odd ghost will make me feel quite a home."

Leo and Lucinda drove Em to church in Leo's car. "Makes a nice change from Lucinda's buggy," Em remarked as she climbed slowly into the back seat.

"There's gratitude." Lucinda snorted. "You never complained before."

"I'm not complaining now, but you must admit it's a sight more comfortable than your jalopy." Em ran her work-worn hand over the velvet upholstery. "I always did have a soft spot for a Buick."

"It's a rented car," he told her. "I usually rent my mobility."

But he wasn't renting Heron Cottage; he was buying it, which meant he would become a fixture in Small Port—at least for part of the year. A little song seemed to start in Lucinda's heart, as she hastily climbed into the front seat, knocking her straw hat off in the process.

"I hope I'm suitably dressed," said Leo, who was wearing beige cotton pants and a dazzling white shirt.

"It's only a small country church, not a cathedral," Lucinda told him.

"Just like Sussex. Lucinda keeps apologizing for her surroundings," he said to Em, "but she forgets I'm a country boy, too. Just a different country, that's all."

"I'm not apologizing," Lucinda protested.

He patted her on the knee. "Don't get cross, darling."

"There's no need to put on an act in front of Em," Lucinda said. "She knows everything. And I'll thank you to keep your hands to yourself."

Leo was as big a hit at church as he'd been at the dance the night before. After the service he insisted on chatting with Em's friends, and Lucinda knew that before long several of the village's more avid gossips would be speculating about her wedding day.

Finally she managed to pry Em away, and Leo drove them home. "I'll be back in a couple of hours," he said, "for tennis."

She'd forgotten about the tennis in her concern about the gossip. Lord, this was going to be a Sunday to remember!

After she'd put the dirty dishes into the dishwasher for Em, she dashed upstairs to change into her new blue shorts, which were much nicer than her tennis whites.

Leo was waiting in the hall when she returned, lounging against the oak settle and swinging his racket lazily. Her heart gave a surprising double flip. He had such strong, straight legs, brown as teak, and she could see the ripple of muscles through the cotton knit of his tennis shirt. The double flip traveled from her heart to her stomach.

Charles came out of the living room and caught sight of his daughter. "What the hell do you think you're wearing?" he asked.

She mumbled, "Sh-shorts."

"We're going to play *tennis*, for God's sake! I'm not having you on the courts dressed like that." Charles prided himself on being a stickler for the proprieties.

"It doesn't really matter, does it, Charlie?" Fran placated.

Trish chimed in, "She's not going to play, Dad."

Charles glared at her. "She'll be on the court, won't she? Besides, Gina's coming. She'll need a partner."

"Not me, surely," said Lucinda, going pale, for Gina was a crack player.

"Not you," Charles agreed, "but I don't see why one of us should sit around without a partner just because you're too lazy to pick up a racket. It'll do you good to play some tennis—get some of the fat off you."

Cheeks burning, Lucinda stole a glance at Leo. He was leaning against the wall, his brilliant eyes hooded.

"I'll go and change," she muttered, unaccustomed hatred for Charles surging in her breast.

In her room she pulled on the hated tennis whites. These shorts, purchased by Fran, were made of heavy poplin, and Lucinda felt as if she were wearing a tent. She looked like it, too, she decided, gazing disconsolately in the mirror. They added inches to her hips. She found her tennis racket, neglected at the back of her closet, and fixed a sweatband around her forehead.

The afternoon was turning out to be even worse than she'd anticipated.

The local tennis courts were within walking distance, and Charles and Fran had left as soon as Lucinda went upstairs to change, but Leo and Trish were still in the hall.

"At last!" said Trish. "Can we please go now?" She bounced out the front door.

Leo held the door for Lucinda. "No wonder your family calls you Cindy," he said. "You've got a regular Cinderella complex."

She bristled. "And just what's that?"

"A Cinderella complex is when a girl is put upon by her relatives but does nothing about it. She just waits passively for her fairy godmother to come and rescue her."

"One thing's for sure, you're no Prince Charming," she said, glaring at him.

He shrugged and went out to join Trish, who was swiping at a flowering bush with her racket in her impatience. They set off, Lucinda trailing behind them.

Looking at those two elegant backs, Trish's red hair so compatible with Leo's gray, she was filled with depression. It was possible that when this farce between Leo and Lucinda was over, he would start an affair with Trish, after all. She was much more his type. Feeling bleaker than ever, Lucinda plodded doggedly along in the glorious sunshine.

Gina didn't arrive for a while, so Lucinda kept score as originally planned. It went fairly well, although there were the usual squabbles with Charles whenever Lucinda declared that a ball was out.

"With your eyesight it's a miracle you can see a tennis ball at all," he declared with an unhumorous laugh after one particularly heated discussion.

Leo didn't say a word but stood by the net, looking at her intently, aloof and disdainful. The way he had been in the old days, when he first came to Small Port.

When Gina finally arrived, she was paired with Leo to play doubles against Trish and Fran, and Charles dragged Lucinda off to a neighboring court to practice her serve. By then she was so disheartened she was practically incapable of holding her racket, much to her father's chagrin. This torture only came to an end when she tripped and fell, grazing her knees on the hard clay surface.

"It's hopeless," Charles declared. "You're unteachable."

"Here!" Leo pushed a clean handkerchief through the wire mesh. "Clean your knees."

"I'm all right," said Lucinda, vowing silently, *I won't cry. I will not cry!*

"This game's nearly over," Leo said. "Then we'll get away on our own."

Gina called, "Come *on*, partner! Save the necking for later." He threw her a look that would have made a less insensitive woman quail.

In spite of the others' protests at the end of his set, Leo refused to play anymore, and he and Lucinda walked back to Cliff Top. There she cleaned up her knees and changed into a yellow cotton dress.

"Much damage done?" he asked when she joined him downstairs.

"No...no. I'm fine...it's hardly anything... well, not much, anyway. I mean...I'll live," she babbled. Being alone with him in the empty house was causing her to feel peculiarly jumpy, and she agreed immediately when he suggested they go for a swim.

"If you feel like it, of course," he said.

"Saltwater's good for scratches," she assured him. "Let's take a thermos of coffee with us."

She boiled the kettle and put some chocolate chip cookies in a bag. "Ah! The owl's back," said Leo, coming into the kitchen. He held her by the shoulders and looked at her closely, and her heart quickened. "Different kind of owl, though," he added, for she was wearing new, rimless glasses. "Very nice."

"Not a vulnerable species this time?" She broke away to pour hot water over the coffee powder.

"I wouldn't say that." He put a small flight bag, containing his towel and sunglasses, onto the counter and watched her while she packed up their modest picnic. She spilled some milk.

"Please don't watch me," she said. "I drop things when I'm being watched."

"You drop things anyway, darling," he said, and she colored.

"It's no fun, being naturally awkward."

"It's no crime, either." His long firm mouth twitched in a smile. "It's preferable to being naturally bitchy."

"I want it all," she admitted ruefully. "I want to be graceful and nice."

"I think you should settle for nice."

He reached for her hand, but she eluded him and said quickly, "Do you want to go to Indian Head, or somewhere else?"

"Why not go to my beach?" he suggested.

"It's not your beach yet," she reminded him, "and it's called Heron Cove."

"Shall we take my car?"

She shook her head. "We don't need a car. There's a way through the woods. Come on!"

It was late in the afternoon when they made their way through the thick spruce forest, and the sun had turned from white-hot silver to old gold. It was cool under the trees, and the evergreen scent filled the still air. A jay screeched high above them and Lucinda started.

"Some folk say that's the cry of a drowned sailor," she said, "but I guess you're much too sensible to believe in stuff like that."

He looked down at her with mock severity. "Then you guess wrong. I'm a Sussex man. We treat ghosts with respect."

"Then you'll love the graveyard," she said. When he looked puzzled, she explained, "There's an old graveyard by the swamp ahead."

"A swamp, too? My cup runneth over. How about mosquitoes?"

She laughed. "Plenty of those. Did you bring any insect repellent?" He shook his head, his hair bright pewter in the sunlight. "We'll be eaten alive then," she promised.

Soon the trees thinned, and to their left was the swamp, covered with water lilies and buzzing with insects. In the middle of a tangle of grasses stood an imposing granite tombstone.

"What have we here?" asked Leo. "Let's take a look."

"Your legs are bare," she warned him. "You'll be bitten to death."

"So will you. Come on, let's risk it."

They pushed their way through the long grass, being bitten with every step, but Lucinda didn't care. At that moment she would have walked through a swamp full of crocodiles, for the afternoon had turned from nightmare to magic, and even crocodiles would not harm her.

Closer inspection revealed about a dozen tombstones hidden in the long grass.

"Look!" said Leo, bending down to examine two little marble cherubs that stood lopsided in the damp earth. One was engraved at the base with the name *Alice*. He scraped at the dirt on the base of the second, and soon they could make out *Anny*.

"The twins' graves," whispered Lucinda, her dark eyes wide.

He looked up. "Twins?"

"Anny and Alice Sinclair. They were ten years old when they drowned in one of the pools near here." She spoke softly, as if afraid the little ghosts might take fright.

He slapped at his neck where a particularly hungry mosquito was biting him. "When was this?"

"Sometime in the 1830s." She knelt in the long ferns and touched the cherub's chiseled curls. "They say you can hear their laughter sometimes. It means..."

"What?"

"It means you've found your one true love," she finished in a rush.

"Have you ever heard them?"

She stood up, pulling at her skirt. "Not yet. We'd better get going if we want to swim before dark."

He led the way back to the path, holding out his hand for hers. "I can hear the surf," he said. "We must be nearly there."

"Nearly. You should be able to see the roof of Heron Cottage on your right. You're tall enough."

He craned his neck in the direction she'd indicated. "So I can. The graveyard's practically at my back door. That makes Anny and Alice my own private ghosts. What a bonus!"

"Maybe Mrs. Bosco won't sell," she warned him.

"Of course she will. Heron Cottage is as good as mine. It's preordained."

Lucinda laughed. "If you say so!"

They reached the beach and she took off her yellow dress. Like Leo, she was wearing a bathing suit under her clothes. They put a smooth stone on their things and waded into the tumbling waves. The beach fell away steeply and she was quickly out of her depth. It was wonderful. Like swimming in champagne! She loved playing in the water like this, diving through the breakers, being turned this way and that by the roaring, singing sea.

After awhile they struck out for the rocks at the far side of the beach. Leo was a powerful swimmer, but he held back to match Lucinda's slower pace. The tide was going out, leaving the sides of the barnacled granite dripping and sharp as a razor, but he found a smooth section and carefully hauled himself up. He held out his hand to Lucinda, who was dog-paddling cautiously in his wake.

"I'm not sure I want to," she told him. When she was younger, she'd climbed after Trish and Gina onto rocks like this, and slipped and gashed her leg. She still remembered the stinging pain...and Gina's vexation.

"I'll help you up," he promised. "If you watch where you put your feet, it's quite safe."

Not wanting to look too timid—particularly after her performance on the tennis court—she swam closer and put her hands into his strong ones. It was a bit slippery, for there was seaweed clinging to the rocks, but with Leo holding her hands she felt safe, and soon he had pulled her up beside him.

He didn't let her go immediately, but held her in a loose embrace. His brown skin was cool against hers, and water drops glistened like crystals in the dark mat of hair on his chest.

"You see," he murmured into her wet curls, "there's nothing to it when you relax."

Rather loudly she said, "What a view!" and eased herself out of his arms. She was sure he must be able to hear her heart, which seemed to be pounding as loudly as the surf.

The view was indeed spectacular. They could see around the edge of the cove, and a ribbon of white breakers stretched into a seemingly endless curve.

Fine lines webbed the corners of Leo's eyes as he creased them against the sun. "What's it like here in winter?"

She laughed. "Cold! I wouldn't want to stand here in January." In winter, snow would drift across the sand and the spume would glitter with ice. "Is it very different from Sussex?"

"Very." He lifted his head, showing the strong column of his neck. "Mind you, we get some fine storms on the channel, but the coast is mostly built up. It's been tamed by man."

He wouldn't like that. Tameness didn't match his personality, for in spite of his elegance there was a wildness in him. That was what made him so attractive, that hint of savagery under the veneer. Standing half-naked on this rock, his powerful body gleaming with water, he seemed all masculine strength and hardness. He reminded her of a picture she'd seen of an early settler, one of a breed of iron men. She gave a little shiver, and he said, "Time to go back, you're getting cold."

They swam side by side, easily riding the crests of foam, the cold clear water dark beneath them. Back on shore the coarse sand felt cool, and she was glad to get dressed and pull a light wool jacket over her shoulders. Leo didn't seem to feel the evening chill, however. He was so alive, so vital, she doubted that he ever felt the cold.

Sitting on a weathered log to drink their coffee, they watched the sun slowly sink into the sea.

"You know," said Leo, taking a sip of hot coffee, "you're a fraud, Lucinda Wainwright. I gather from the family chat that you're a dud at sports."

She passed him the bag of cookies. "You saw for yourself on the tennis court," she said. The memory of that scene dimmed the sunset a little.

"Yet you swim like a fish."

"A very slow fish."

"Who cares?" He took a cookie. "These biscuits look good. Did you bake them?"

"Cookies!" She wriggled her bare toes in the sand. "My father cares."

"That's your father's problem. I think you try too hard to please him, Lucinda."

"He wouldn't agree with you. He doesn't think I try at all."

"Your father's a good artist," said Leo, "but that doesn't make him a good parent."

That might be true, but she couldn't admit it. That would be disloyal. "Life hasn't always been easy for him," she said. But while she spoke she knew that wasn't true. Charles had always been cosseted by his women. "You have to make allowances for artists," she insisted.

He ran his finger down her cheek. "Your father's a lucky man, having you on his team."

His touch, light as sea foam, flustered her, and she moved a millimeter away from him. "I guess we'd better be going," she whispered.

When they got to their feet, he put his hand under her hair and caressed the nape of her neck, and she was suddenly searingly happy. His face was tinted red-brown by the last faint light of the setting sun, and his eyes blazed blue. She was unable to move. Being hypnotized must feel like this, she thought, and then he kissed her full on the mouth and drove every thought out of her head.

CHAPTER SEVEN

SHE COULDN'T HAVE MOVED even if she'd wanted to...but she didn't want to. He tasted of salt, and sun, and clean attractive man. As his tongue gently probed her mouth, delicious little tremors ran all through her. Without taking his lips from hers he pivoted her slightly sideways and put his hand over one of her breasts, and a slow sweet fire started to burn deep in her. Flames leaped to life in the most secret untouched part of her body. It was heaven.... It was madness! She pulled her mouth from his.

"No! Stop. Please. Stop, Leo."

He looked down at her in the dusk, his eyes glazed with desire. "Don't tell me you don't like it."

"That's not the point," she said, desperately pushing his hand away.

He pulled her roughly back into his arms. "Why don't we make the rumor a reality?" he whispered huskily. "No more playacting."

She pushed at his broad chest, which was about as effective as trying to stop a truck with her bare hands. "Let go of me, Leo. Please!"

Reluctantly he did. "I'm sorry, Lucinda. I didn't plan that." He took a shuddering breath. "Though why I should apologize because I find you over-whelmingly attractive, I don't know."

"Attractive is one thing," she said, kneeling down to fasten her sandal, "jumping on me is something else. You seem to have forgotten you said rape wasn't your style."

"I object to 'jumping'," he said. "I did no such thing. I suppose it would be ungentlemanly of me to point out that you seemed to be thoroughly enjoying yourself?"

She said stiffly, "I don't think you're in any posi-tion to talk about gentlemen."

"Oh, come off it, darling! I've apologized, don't make a federal case of it."

She was making too much of it, she knew that. But the ardor his touch had unleashed frightened her. She had not known she was capable of such intensity.

"Maybe it's perfectly okay to go around mauling girls where you come from," she flared at him, "but here in Small Port we don't go for that sort of stuff."

There was a dead, sick pause. "I'm sorry you felt mauled," he said coldly. "It won't happen again."

Fool, fool! screamed her heart, but all she said was, "It had better not."

They walked back silently on either side of the track, but the space between them could have been a mile wide. When they reached the old graveyard the moon rose, flooding the marsh with light and haloing the bulrushes with a nimbus of silver. If she hadn't been so cross she would have taken his arm, for the night was full of strange whispers, but she didn't intend to give him any kind of encouragement, and so she plodded on unaided.

He looked across at her, stumbling along in the moonlight. "We must remember to bring a torch next time."

"Flashlight!" she growled, and quickened her pace.

"What time do you finish work tomorrow?" he asked when they reached the house.

Lucinda, who had been preparing herself to refuse his invitation to dinner that evening, was caught off guard. She stammered, "F-five-thirty."

"I'll pick you up at five-thirty then," he said, and roared off without even bothering to find out if it was convenient. Not that it mattered whether it was or not, she supposed, since she'd agreed to be at his disposal.

That was going to change pretty fast, if he continued behaving like a British Casanova every five minutes.

Sunday was Em's evening off, and she and the rest of the family were out. Lucinda made herself a peanut butter sandwich, and after watching television for an hour decided to go to bed early. She might as well have watched the late movie, because sleep refused to come. She tossed and turned for what seemed like hours, and finally drifted off into an uneasy dream in which Leo kept trying to kiss her through the mesh of a gigantic tennis racket.

Just after five the following afternoon the head librarian looked up from checking over a list of new books with Lucinda, and said, "Now, *that's* what I call a nice-looking man!" Lucinda looked up, too, and saw Leo, leafing through a newspaper in the corner where they kept the magazines.

"Oh Lord!" she said. "He's early."

Miss Phipps might have been close to retirement, but she still had an eye for an attractive man. She patted her blue-rinsed hair and asked, "Is that your English friend, Lucinda? He looks delightful. Introduce me, dear." She beamed, her false teeth flashing like traffic signals. "I've heard so much about him."

Lucinda didn't doubt that. Ethel Phipps was part of a group of formidable elderly ladies who exchanged gossip as often as some people exchanged their library books. Reluctantly Lucinda beckoned Leo over, and Miss Phipps simpered girlishly and kept hold of his hand.

Lucinda muttered something about finishing the list of new books before she quit for the day.

"I think that can wait until tomorrow, dear. You can leave early." Miss Phipps giggled impishly. "I guess you'll be leaving us altogether soon."

"I can't imagine why I'd do that," said Lucinda, red in the face. Miss Phipps gurgled. "Listen to little Miss Innocent!"

"I'll be thankful when the old bat retires," Lucinda said to Leo when they were outside. "I think she's going senile."

"She does seem to suffer from a certain lubricious curiosity," he said, holding the car door open.

She climbed into the passenger seat. "It's a good thing I'm familiar with dictionaries. Do you always have to use twenty-dollar words?"

"Yes, it's the way I am." He twisted around to scrutinize her. "I don't intend to change myself just to please others. You might try it."

She bristled. "Are we going someplace? Or am I here for a lecture?"

"You are here because I asked you to be," he replied. "But first I want to talk."

She peered around the parking lot. "Isn't this rather public?"

"There's nobody around, and what I have to say won't take long." His brows came together in a frown.

Oh, God! thought Lucinda, *he's going to tell me to get lost. Please, please don't let him do that.*

"It's about yesterday," he said. "I behaved badly and I'm sorry."

It was a good thing she was sitting down, for relief made her legs weak. "You already apologized," she reminded him.

"Not very well." He took one of her hands, which she'd clasped tightly together, and held it in both of his. "I'll try and do a better job now. I'm sorry, Lucinda, and I promise to try not to...not to jump on you...again."

She looked up at him, eyes glowing. "You didn't really jump...and I did enjoy it."

He gave a rough chuckling laugh, and squeezed her hand. "I'm not going to promise never to kiss you again," he said softly. "That would be utterly impos-

sible. But I won't do anything you don't want.
Agreed?''

It suddenly seemed like the Fourth of July, with
skyrockets going off in her heart. She asked, "What
do you mean, 'utterly impossible'?''

"You seem to have that effect on me. I keep wanting to kiss you all the time." To prove these words he
moved his head closer and lightly brushed her lips with
his.

"Oh!'' she murmured, and then, "Watch out!'' for
Miss Phipps had come out of the building and was
tripping toward her car. She waggled her fingers at
Lucinda.

"A graceful exit is indicated," said Leo, turning the
key in the ignition. "I thought we'd go somewhere nice
and have dinner." He grinned. "Mea culpa for yesterday.''

They ate at a waterside restaurant that was justly
famous for its seafood. Seated at a table in the
screened patio, they could see the light from Fish-
pond Island flashing intermittently over an ocean that
was as smooth as ivory.

"Let's start with some steamers, shall we," said
Leo, scrutinizing the menu, "followed by Lobster
Mornay? That should keep us going for a bit."

"Is it an English custom, this passion for shell-
fish?'' Lucinda teased. "That, and buying broken-
down houses?'' She took a hot roll from the basket he
offered, smiling at him. She'd been smiling ever since
he'd told her he wanted to kiss her all the time. She felt
there was a unity growing between them, like—like the

hedge of wild roses at Heron Cottage. Sweet, and delicate, and as yet, fragile as spun sugar.

"You like old buildings, too," he said. "Don't I remember Trish accusing you of being a nut about local history?"

"The state of Heron Cottage is enough to deter an antiquarian," she told him.

"When it's fixed up it'll be a showcase," he promised, pouring wine into her glass. His hands were deft and capable. He had large, strong hands, but she knew they could be gentle. They had been gentle when he held her on the rocks at Heron Cove. It would be wonderful to feel his touch again. To feel his caresses . . .

The waiter brought their clams. "Bang goes my diet." Lucinda grinned. "I'll have to fast for the next couple of days."

"What rubbish! You've got a lovely figure."

"Dad doesn't share your opinion. You heard him this afternoon." The smile had faded from her lips.

"You always quote your father," Leo observed. "Don't you remember your mother at all?"

"Vaguely. I was five when she died. She was little and plump, and . . . *cuddly*, I do remember that."

"Like you," he said. "You're the cuddliest thing I've ever met."

"You make me sound like a puppy." She hurried on. "It's funny, really, that Dad chose someone like my mother, because he doesn't like little women. He likes 'em tall and thin, like Fran. Poor old Dad! He wanted his child to be like him and instead he got a carbon copy of his wife. It's lucky that Trish and Gina are the kind of girls he likes. It makes up a little for his disappointment."

He looked at her, his fork poised. "His disappointment?"

"Me! I've never measured up."

"You're not eating your clams," said Leo, and obediently she dipped one into the dish of melted butter. "Your father's not from around here, is he?"

"He's from New York. He came here for a painting vacation and never went back."

"And married your mother."

"Yes, it was a whirlwind courtship."

"If she was like you I can understand it."

She deliberately ate another clam before saying, "Personally, I don't trust whirlwind courtships. Em won't talk about it, but I don't think they were happy. I remember Mom crying a lot, and Dad hollering at her. She always seemed kind of sad."

"That's a hard thing for a little girl to deal with," Leo said quietly.

"Oh! There were happy times, too." But she had more sad than happy memories of her mother.

"Go on," he encouraged.

"There's not much to tell, really. Dad married Fran within a year of Mom's death...*that* was hard for me. But I was just a kid. I didn't understand, I guess."

"And his marriage to Fran's a success, I take it."

"A roaring success. Even though she doesn't have any money."

She bit her lip. A thought she had always shied away from was the conviction that Charles Wainwright had only married her mother for convenience. For what could have been more fortuitous for a penniless artist than to meet an unworldly orphan who had a house of her own and valuable land to go with it. "I know you can't force love, but..." She gave a little sigh and then smiled ruefully. "You'll think twice before you ask me out to dinner again. I didn't mean to unload on you."

"I'm glad you did." He smiled, his eyes tender in the glow of the candles. "Very glad."

Their lobster arrived and the conversation turned to other topics. Lucinda wondered how she could have talked about her past like that—and to a stranger! Except that Leo wasn't a stranger anymore, he was a friend. Her mind skidded away from the possibility of more than friendship. Friendship was what she wanted. Friendship was plenty. But when she said good-night and he put his hands on either side of her face, she relaxed her mouth, waiting for his kiss.

He merely brushed her forehead with his lips in a brotherly way. "Do you think you might talk that gushy boss of yours into giving you a couple of days off this week?" he asked. "I'd like to go and see Mrs. Bosco, and get Heron Cottage settled." Lucinda said she would ask, and hoped that now he'd kiss her properly, but he simply said, "Fine!" and got back into the car.

Miss Phipps readily agreed to give Lucinda Wednesday and Thursday off. "You can make up the time later, dear," she said. After all, Lucinda Wainwright had rarely asked for time off and had always been willing to stand in for one or another of her colleagues. She had earned a couple of days for herself.

Wednesday was another perfect day, and Lucinda had a holiday feeling as she packed the picnic lunch Em insisted she take.

"You don't want to be eating some bought muck, when there's food to spare here," she said, tucking a jar of pickles into the cooler. "See that Abigail gets these." She grinned. "She's no hand at making pickles. Makes her real mad that mine turn out so good."

The screen door banged and Fran, sweat-suited and hot from her morning jog, came into the kitchen. She looked at Lucinda's poppy-trimmed sun hat, which was balanced on the cooler. "What's this? Aren't you going to work?"

"Leo and I are going to Vermont to see the woman who owns Heron Cottage."

"And are you coming back tonight?" Fran asked, pointedly eyeing Lucinda's overnight bag standing on the floor.

"Of course not. It's much too far," Lucinda said airily.

"I declare, I don't know what's happened to young people," Fran said to no one in particular. "My daddy would have locked me in my room on bread and water if I'd taken off with a man without so much as a by-your-leave."

"People of the opposite sex do go on vacations together these days, Fran. It doesn't necessarily mean they're leaping into bed."

Fran looked at her with mournful eyes. "After your night on Marshall's Island I'm not foolish enough to think your involvement with Leo is platonic, honey," she said. Not in a position to deny the adventure, Lucinda remained silent. "I don't want to spoil your fun, Cindy," Fran continued. "I can see that for a girl like you, being romanced by someone like Leo is pretty exciting—"

"But you don't want me to get hurt," Lucinda finished for her.

Aware that she was repeating herself, Fran bridled. "It's not only you I'm worried about," she insisted. "What about your daddy? If you go on like this, you're going to break his heart."

"Don't be ridiculous, Fran. Dad only notices me when I fall over."

"Wait till you present him with a bastard. He'll notice you then," her stepmother promised. She suddenly appeared to see Em, who was pretending to search for a jar of preserves in the pantry. "We won't discuss this anymore, not in front of the servants. There's been enough gossip already." She raised her voice. "Mr. Wainwright would like French toast for his breakfast, please, Em," and she slammed from the room.

"Too bad you have to take the lectures an' not get any of the fun," said Em, coming out of the pantry. She fixed Lucinda with an eagle eye. "Or are you?"

"Not that kind of fun." She deliberately changed the subject. Holding her hat against the skirt of her purple-and-white-striped cotton dress, she asked, "Do you think these clash?"

"They're fine," said Em. "Now, if you've got any sense you'll go outside and wait for Mr. Grosvenor before anyone else gets down an' starts in on you. No point spoiling your holiday."

Lucinda agreed, and when Leo arrived she was standing by the front gate waiting for him. "Is this just eagerness to get started, or are you trying to keep me away from your family?" he inquired.

She made a face, wrinkling her nose. "Let's just say that the family—or certain members—are rather heavy going this morning."

"Let's put this in the boot," he said, taking the cooler.

"In the what?" She giggled.

"The boot—the luggage compartment." He opened the trunk. "In here!"

"We need a phrase book," she sighed. "We speak different languages."

"We don't, darling. We just use different words." He slammed the trunk shut. "Our hearts speak the same language."

She felt as if she were being wrapped in a cloak of love, safe and secure forever. Only she wasn't safe, of course. Not from him or from herself.

Leo suggested she choose some music, and the yearning sounds of a Rodrigo concerto for the harp floated out from the tape deck as they left the turnpike and headed away from the coast. Now the smell of the sea was replaced by the scent of earth, lakes and resin. Tilting roads wound up through hills covered with late-summer foliage. As they started to climb, the foothills were left behind them and the mountain range loomed ahead—a broken wall of granite.

"Some of those mountains are nearly three million years old," Lucinda mused, sniffing the sharp mountain air like a puppy. "It's just the people that are new. They came after the glaciers."

He grinned. "Quite a bit after. Watch for a nice place to picnic, I'm starving."

They found a perfect spot where a stream tumbled over a shelf of rock, and slabs of granite rimmed a pool below. Sunlight glinted off the dark green water. The scenery seemed to add flavor to Em's fried chicken and sourdough biscuits, and Lucinda and Leo attacked the food hungrily, leaning back against the schisted rocks, content with the world. There was fruit to finish, and Em had included a thermos of apple juice as well as black coffee for Leo.

"That was delicious," Leo said, putting orange peel into a plastic garbage bag. "And now I'm going to look over some papers for half an hour with my coffee."

She paddled in the pool while he did this. The water felt like silk on her ankles and was crystal clear. Soon she noticed the paper drooping in Leo's hand and his head nodding, and she crept up out of the water and lay on her back beside the pool, lazily watching some yellow butterflies darting around a bush....

Something tickled her chin and she woke with a start. Leo was standing over her, stroking her face with a daisy.

"I couldn't find any buttercups," he said, "or I'd ask you if you like butter."

He seemed to tower above her from where she lay. He was brown from the sun, and his skin looked like coffee with the merest dash of cream in it. His pale blue shirt was open, and she could see that the black hair on his chest was threaded slightly with silver. She felt a pang of desire for him that was as sharp as the prick of a needle.

Scrambling to her feet, she said, "I ... I must have fallen asleep."

"Take it easy, darling. We've only slept half an hour." He put his hand on her shoulder, and it was all she could do not to fling herself into his arms. Misunderstanding her reaction, he said, "Relax, Lucinda. I gave you my word that I wouldn't try to make love to you. I won't break it."

For a moment she could find it in her heart to regret his sterling integrity, for she wanted to feel his strong arms around her, his lips teasing and caressing hers....

She took the black-eyed Susan from him, broke off the stem and floated the flower out onto the surface of the pool. "A thank-you to the gods," she said, "for helping us find this lovely spot."

"Maybe you should send a bunch of flowers to the cartographer too," he suggested. "This place is marked on the map."

She laughed. "Cynic!" she said as they returned to the car. The moment of sensuality had evaporated with their laughter, but she was still aware of an exciting...expectancy. As if she were balanced on the very brink of fulfillment.

They arrived in Mrs. Bosco's village in the late afternoon. "I think the first thing we should do is find a place to stay," said Leo. "Then I can phone her to make an appointment."

"About tonight." She cleared her throat. For the past hour or so the question of hotel accommodation had been bothering her. Sharing his bed on Marshall's Island when she'd heartily disliked him was one thing, but to repeat the experiment now was out of the question, for she was beginning to realize that even sitting close to him was like a powerful drug. If they were lying together on a bed—the very idea made her head spin. "I do want my own room," she said firmly.

"Oh ye of little faith!" he said, gently touching the tip of her nose.

They decided to stay at a private house that did bed and breakfast instead of a motel. "We don't seem to be lucky with motels," said Leo wryly.

The people who ran the guest house had two rooms free. Lucinda was given a large bedroom, charmingly decorated in almond, green and white, with a four-poster bed and a gleaming walnut dresser. There was also an adjoining green bathroom with a door leading to another room. Cautiously she tried the handle. The door opened to reveal a bedroom that was a twin to hers, except the bed was an antique brass one. There was a Windsor chair by the window, too, and Leo was seated in it, looking very much at home.

"Oh!" said Lucinda. "We share a bathroom, do we?"

"Just like old times," he said. "Why don't you have a leisurely bath while I visit Mrs. Bosco. I can't settle till I've seen her and Heron Cottage is mine."

"Do you never admit the possibility that for once you might not get what you want?" Lucinda wondered aloud.

He looked at her intently. "I'm beginning to think I'll die if I don't get some of the things I want."

"Heron Cottage isn't the only house in Small Port, you know," she reminded him.

He paused for a moment before saying, "Heron Cottage?" he seemed to mentally shake himself. "No, of course not."

After he'd gone, bearing Em's jar of pickles as an introductory gift, she washed away the grime of the day's journey and changed into her lilac sun dress, which she teamed up with a neat little white piqué jacket, for late-summer evenings in Vermont can be cool.

She waited for him in the garden, on the flagstoned patio, enjoying the scent from a clump of nicotiana, flowering tobacco plant, and watching the swallows dip and wheel against the sky. It had been such a great day! The scenic drive, their picnic—but she knew that it wasn't the scenery or the picnic that filled her with this singing happiness. It was because of Leo that she felt this heady mixture of excitement and security.

There was no point hiding the truth from herself any longer. She was falling in love with him.

She reached out and touched a hanging basket of red geraniums, and some petals fell and scattered at her feet like pieces of scarlet confetti. What was the matter with that? She was a free agent, and so was he. And he was attracted to her. "Why don't we make the rumor a reality?" he'd said. All she had to do tonight was tap on his door and he would welcome her.

It would be sweet, so sweet, to be loved by him. Sweet to sleep in his arms afterward. You might almost say that fate had decreed it, to make up for their ghastly night on Marshall's Island....

That brought her up with a start. The rumors that had grown from that adventure were the reason she was here now. Here to repay a favor. Held in a kind of bondage until he saw fit to free her. Except the past week hadn't been bondage, it had been fun, and Leo was quickly becoming far more than a man to whom she owed a moral debt.

She collected the fallen geranium petals. They lay in her palm like drops of blood, and she carefully put them in an ashtray on a garden table. What if this sense of intimacy between them was nothing more to him than the beginning of a casual summer affair, a diversion until he returned to England? Returned to his manor house, and his life there. A life that was a far cry from anything Lucinda knew. How would she feel then? She could put on an act for her family, pretend that she'd had a lovely romance that was now over and no harm done. But she knew that if she were foolish enough to melt into his arms, the sense of rejection she would suffer when he left her would scar her for life. The very thought of such pain made her shiver, and she went back into the house to wait for him.

She was sitting on a chair in the hall when he came back, her huge dark eyes somber. "Heron Cottage is mine!" he cried triumphantly. "Mrs. Bosco was delighted to sell. She's even given me the keys, so I can move in whenever I want."

"Congratulations," she said quietly. There would be no escaping him now. This net of love was closing tighter.

"And," he said, "she gave me this." He held aloft a basket she'd not noticed before.

"What is it?" It seemed to move with a life of its own.

"She breeds cats. Her place is crawling with them. I admired this kitten and she insisted I take him. She said it was to be our first wedding present."

CHAPTER EIGHT

"WHAT ARE YOU TALKING about?" she gasped.

"Mrs. Bosco seemed convinced I wanted to buy Heron Cottage because I was about to marry you and settle down." He grinned. "Nothing I said seemed to change her mind."

"Where on earth would she get such an idea?" demanded Lucinda, cheeks burning.

"I gather she hears from Small Point from time to time. It would appear that gossip travels. But darling, don't look so stricken. You're not going to be forced to prove her right."

She managed a weak smile, although smiling wasn't really what she felt like at all.

"Now let's take a look at our cat," Leo suggested. "Mrs. Bosco tells me he's a Maine coon."

"That cat has nothing to do with me," Lucinda insisted. The mewing from the basket seemed to grow louder. "It's your responsibility."

"Hard-hearted female!" Carefully he lifted the lid. Two odd-colored eyes set in an indignant ginger face glared up at them. "What a handsome fellow," Leo crooned, putting out a finger to scratch the animal's square head. A heavily tufted paw, claws extended, shot out.

"Bad-tempered fellow, too," commented Lucinda.

"You'd be bad-tempered if you'd just been wrenched away from your home," said Leo.

She paused for a second before murmuring, "No, I wouldn't!"

"What are we going to call him?" Leo closed the lid.

"We are not going to call him anything." She rapped on the lid of the box. "Stop that noise!"

"Well, we'll worry about his name later. Right now we must find him something to eat."

Fortunately there were cats at the guest house, and the kitten was soon provided with food, milk and an improvised litter box made from a disposable roasting pan. This seen to, they left him in Leo's bedroom and went in search of dinner for themselves.

"Are you aware that Maine coons grow into giants?" said Lucinda, when they were sitting at a local steak house waiting for their food. "Some folk claim they're part raccoon."

"Well, I'm not calling him 'Rocky'," said Leo. "Too obvious."

"Why not call him Boots?" suggested Lucinda. "As in Bossy Boots. I think it suits him. He looks the bossy type."

He held up his glass of Californian Burgundy. "Here's to Boots. May he have a long and happy life."

"I'm sure he will." She sipped the velvety wine. "He strikes me as a very determined cat."

"You do realize that he's half yours," Leo pointed out, "in spite of your protests."

"He was given to you."

"He was given to both of us. And what's going to happen to him when I'm in England? He can't fend for himself."

"I guess you'll just have to find another home for him," she said firmly. "It's not practical for you to have a cat."

Their steaks arrived, thick and sizzling. Leo put a spoonful of mustard on the side of his plate. "Don't you like cats, Lucinda?"

"I like all animals." She remembered a marmalade kitten her father had insisted she give away. 'I don't want a bunch of animals underfoot,' he'd said. Fran had tried to get him to change his mind, but it had been useless.

"So what's the problem?" His keen blue eyes searched her face.

"Maybe we can hide him in the kitchen," she said. "Just as long as he doesn't get under Dad's feet."

Leo speared a french fry on the end of his fork. "Doesn't your father like cats?"

"Well, I had one once, and…" She told him about getting rid of her marmalade kitten.

He looked at her judicially. "And did this sacrifice pay off? Was your father grateful?"

She eyed him warily. There was a muscle twitching in his cheek, and she was learning that this heralded trouble. "Grateful?"

"Yes. Did he love you for giving up your pet? I mean, that's why you did it, isn't it? To make him love you."

She stopped eating, for swallowing suddenly seemed a problem. "He didn't seem to notice."

"And you went back to your chimney corner, I suppose," he said, "and wriggled your toes in the ashes."

She looked away. "I don't know what you're talking about."

"I'm talking about your Cinderella act." He leaned toward her, forcing her to look at him. "I think it's time you changed the pantomime, Lucinda. You're too intelligent for the role."

"What role?"

He put down his fork. "You know very well. You've been playing it all your life. The casting was done for you when Charles married again. Right down to the wicked stepmother."

"Fran isn't wicked," she protested, but Leo wasn't finished.

"Shut up and listen!" he snapped. "I'm not saying you haven't had a rough time. Having a father who doesn't love you is damnable, but why in the name of all that's reasonable, don't you fight back? It's not as if you're incapable of losing your temper. I should know, you fight me often enough."

She bleated, "That's different . . ." but he went on.

"You seem unable to understand that you'll never win your father's love by constantly doing things you hate just to please him. He despises you, Lucinda, and

you're either too stubborn—or too stupid—to see it."
He sawed savagely at his steak.

White to the lips, she said, "I'm sorry you're wasting your time with a fool."

"I don't understand you," he said, regarding her with a kind of resigned ferocity. "Why the hell don't you move out? You're not a child. You don't have to live at home."

"I do, as a matter of fact," she said. "I happen to own the house. My mother left it to me in her will."

He gave her a startled glance before saying. "All right! So Cliff Top is yours. You still don't have to stay there. Houses can be sold. You could start a new life."

She could have told him then about her fears for Em, but she didn't. She was reeling from this unexpected attack. She hadn't been looking for sympathy with her story about the cat, but she hadn't been looking for a quarrel, either.

"I really think you should mind your own business," she said, her voice flat as a slice of bread.

"Friends care about each other," he told her. "I thought we were friends."

"Did you?" The pause that followed these two words felt like an eternity.

She wanted to reach across the table and grasp his strong brown wrists, wanted to plead, "Don't listen to me, Leo... I don't mean what I'm saying." But she couldn't plead with this man. That was the way she behaved with her father, and Charles despised her for it. She couldn't bear for Leo to despise her, too, so all she said was, "This steak's really good," and concentrated on her meal.

Conversation after this was sporadic. Leo asked her to make out a list of contractors in Small Point. "I want to get started on Heron Cottage," he said. Lucinda nodded, and hid the hurt she felt because he seemed suddenly to have excluded her from his plans.

She didn't sleep very well that night. The bed was fresh and comfortable, but it could have been as lumpy as that mattress on Marshall's Island for all the rest she got. Boots didn't help, either. He had been put in the bathroom in his basket, and he showed his resentment by mewing continuously. He finally stopped in the small hours, and at breakfast she discovered that Leo had relented and the kitten had spent the remainder of the night curled up against his back. Lucky cat, she thought wistfully.

During the drive home it clouded over, but it was not the gray skies that depressed her, it was this awful constraint that had come between them, like a stone wall. Quarreling with Leo had been better. At least when they quarreled she felt alive. This caution with each other was a deadly paralysis.

He dropped her off at Cliff Top, grunting that he intended going on to Heron Cottage. She felt absurdly hurt that he wasn't taking her. If it hadn't been for her he wouldn't have found it, and she wanted to be with him when he stepped over the threshold for the first time.

Em was clearing away the dinner dishes when she went into the kitchen. Em looked tired, and Lucinda felt a pang of guilt. "I'll do that," she said, taking the dirty broiler pan out of the old woman's hands.

"The family've gone off to Del's store to look at white-water rafts, so they had dinner early," Em said, easing the shoes off her swollen feet with a sigh. "I saved you a couple of lamb chops."

But Lucinda wasn't hungry. While she scoured the pans she told Em about Leo's purchase of the cottage, and Em smiled wanly, but seemed too tired to make conversation.

"Now," said Lucinda, turning on the dishwasher, "you go on upstairs to bed. I'll bring you a hot drink later."

Em shook her head doubtfully. "Mrs. W. Wants the coffee service cleaned for tomorrow," she said. "She's usin' it for her badminton club's coffee morning."

Lucinda gently pulled the old lady to her feet. "I'll do it." She handed Em her shoes. "Off you go."

"I think I will at that," said Em, and then she reached up and gently stroked Lucinda's cheek, saying, "You're so like your ma . . . so like."

Lucinda got out the silver polish and started on the fluted silver coffee service that had belonged to her mother's family. It wouldn't have hurt Fran to do this herself, she thought as she rubbed away at the oval tray, but Fran was far too busy with her badminton and her tennis to do anything as menial as clean silver. Particularly with a servant around. That reminded Lucinda of Em's tired face, and a small tremor of dread went through her. Well, she would just have to do more to help, that was all. She'd been gadding about too much lately, so maybe it was just as well that things between herself and Leo were cooling off. Now she'd have more time to devote to Em, so it was an ill wind, as the saying went. Nevertheless, when she finally went up to bed herself, it was with a heavy heart.

It grew heavier when the next day Leo didn't get in touch with her. By quitting time she was longing to see him, so when Olga suggested they go out for a meal and a movie she turned her down, although distraction was really what she needed.

"Date with Leo, eh?" said Olga with an understanding grin.

Lucinda shrugged. "I'm not sure. He may be waiting at home."

But he wasn't—and he didn't phone. She killed the time by doing a pile of ironing for Em, and got some minor satisfaction knowing she was lightening Em's work load.

Before she went to bed she walked on Indian Head Beach. It was a dark night, but the rain that had been falling most of the day had stopped, and the wind blowing against her face was fresh. That night she slept well and woke feeling rested, but her heart was as hollow as an empty seashell.

CHAPTER NINE

LEO STAYED AWAY for nearly ten days.

One day she bumped into Ed during her lunch hour and accepted his invitation to join him for a snack. Anything that would keep her from phoning Leo's office. It was worth being bored by poor Ed, if it meant she could hang on to her pride.

They ate at a health food café close to the library. "How's Leo?" Ed asked, when they'd selected sandwiches and were seated at a small table for two.

"Busy." She brushed a crumb off her denim skirt with unnecessary vigor.

"Yeah? Well, I reckon he's a go-getter," Ed observed gloomily. "He's the kind who gets places."

"Bulldozes his way, in fact," said Lucinda, her brown eyes glinting.

Ed brightened. "You had a fight?"

"No." She took a bite of her tuna on whole wheat. It stuck to the roof of her mouth like a piece of flannel. Irritation with Leo seemed to rob her food of texture as well as taste. "I haven't seen much of him lately," she said, her mouth full.

"How come?" Ed was looking happier and happier.

She put the rest of her sandwich back in its paper bag. She'd deal with it during the afternoon. "I told you, he's busy."

The light faded from Ed's face. He blurted, "Are you going to marry him?"

"He hasn't asked me."

"I bet he will." He took a noisy gulp of grape juice.

"When he does I'll see that you're the first to know," she replied tartly.

Ed chewed steadily. "Look, Lucinda," he said finally, "if you and Leo don't...you know... If you do break up...you know that I...that you've got a friend."

"I've got a lot of friends," she said. Ed was getting seriously on her nerves. The contrast between this boy, sitting here swallowing food like an overanxious frog, and Leo was overwhelming. Even when she was mad at Leo she had to admit that he was the most elegant man she'd ever known. And the wittiest. Still, it wasn't Ed's fault that he lacked charisma, and so she added, "I consider you one of them, Ed."

He cheered up after that, but Lucinda didn't. It was suddenly glaringly apparent that when she returned to her old life she would miss the stimulation of Leo's company even more than she'd imagined. He might be arrogant, but he never bored her. The possibility of a future with Ed or someone like him was appalling.

The next few days crept by with the rapidity of a geriatric snail. Then, when she got home on Friday evening, there was Leo, sitting in the living room with her father, a glass of Scotch in his hand. He must have come straight from the office, for he was dressed in a beautifully tailored navy business suit, a half inch of snowy white shirt cuff immaculate against his tanned wrists. He looked as cool as a cucumber, and she was so happy to see him she could have danced—or hit him for appearing unannounced like this.

Unsmilingly he rose to his feet, and she congratulated herself that the emotion she felt didn't show, for she managed to say quite coolly, "Welcome back."

"Leo's agreed to come sailing with us tomorrow," Charles said. "The weather promises to be first-class." This was the first Lucinda had heard about taking *Yankee Doodle* out. Besides, the weather forecast was for high wind and rain. But of course that was the kind of weather intrepid sailors like Leo and her father enjoyed. "Thought we'd try for Portland."

Conscious of Leo's unwavering gaze, she muttered, "That should be nice."

"It'll be a long trip," her father reported gleefully, "so make sure you bring plenty of food."

She regarded him bleakly. "Am I coming, too?"

"What do you think! Trish and Fran will have their hands full crewing. You'll be needed in the galley." Trish and Fran would more than likely be leaning over the side if the weather turned really rough.

"I could make everything ahead. All you'd have to do is heat it," she suggested halfheartedly.

"You haven't been out on *Yankee Doodle* for weeks," Charles accused her. "It won't hurt you to give up one Saturday." She agreed, because she supposed she owed it to him.

Charles got up from his chair. "Leo's taking us all out for dinner tonight," he told his daughter. "I'd better go and hurry Fran up."

"Are you really coming sailing tomorrow?" Leo asked when Charles had left them.

She went to the tall windows that looked over the sea, a slate-colored sea now, roaring with combers. "I guess so."

"Such a dutiful daughter," he said scathingly.

"I didn't have any say in the matter," she muttered.

And Leo declared, "You mean your father would have given you a hard time if you'd refused."

She turned back from looking at those cruel waves. "Yes," she said, "he would."

"Well, you have nothing to worry about. You've been a good little girl...as usual."

She bit back an angry retort. No point quarreling with him now—not within earshot of Fran and her father. "I'd better tell Em she doesn't have to cook dinner," she said, making for the door.

He reached it ahead of her. "I'll come, too. I'd like to say hello." He held the door, and she felt his proximity was fraught with danger, as if she were passing through a mine field. One stumble and she might find herself in his arms, and then, no matter how he might reject her, she would be totally lost.

Em gave Leo a warm welcome, hauling herself out of her chair and wincing a little, for this weather made her rheumatism act up.

"Don't get up, Em," he said, helping the old lady back into her chair. "I only dropped in to say good-evening."

"Aren't you stayin' for supper?" Em asked.

Lucinda told her that he was taking the Wainwright's out to eat. "So you can take it easy tonight, Em. Would you like me to get some of that stew out of the freezer for you?"

Em shook her white head. "Don't bother. A couple of eggs will do me fine."

"Are you sure?" Lucinda looked worried.

"Course I'm sure," snapped Em. "It's my stomach." She pointed a gnarled finger in Lucinda's direction and said to Leo, "This one is the spittin' image of her ma, and she's got the same nature. Miss Lillian was always considerate, an' Lucinda's just the same. Bit too considerate with some, if you ask me."

"Nobody is asking you," Lucinda cut in, but Leo nodded.

"I agree."

"Mind you," Em confided, "I don't know how I'd manage without Lucinda's help. I couldn't do all the work here without her, and if Mrs. W. knew that I was slowing down, she'd give me the push as sure as God made little apples. I'd have to leave, an' I wouldn't like that. I wouldn't feel right any place 'cept Small Port. Besides, Lucinda's like my own, I wouldn't like bein' parted from her."

"It's not going to happen, Em," said Lucinda. "Anyway, I don't do much."

But Em sucked in her cheeks and said, "Oh? And who is it gets up early to do the vacuumin' because I can't manage it anymore? Who cleans the windows, an' clears up after parties?"

"Stop it, Em!" Lucinda said firmly. "I happen to like vacuuming."

"You can tell *that* to the Marines!" the old woman declared, with a triumphant look at Leo.

Not wanting to hear any more of this kind of talk, Lucinda left them and went up to change and hurriedly apply some fresh makeup.

When she returned downstairs Leo had joined the family, including Gina and Del, in the living room for drinks. He looked up when she scurried in, tripping over the edge of the rug in her haste.

She had put on a two-piece dress, one of the few garments Fran had given her that was in a pastel shade—a soft mint green. With its shoulders reduced to gentle curves and the skirt less voluminous, it was now most becoming, and if she'd not been feeling so aggravated by Leo, she might have preened a little. As it was, under his judicial blue gaze she slopped the glass of sherry her father handed her.

"For God's sake, stop that!" Charles snapped when she started mopping at the rug with her handkerchief.

Fran pressed the bell at the side of the fireplace. "Don't get in such a state, honey," she cautioned her husband. "You should be used to Cindy spilling things."

"Dear little Cindy and her handful of thumbs," remarked Gina nastily.

Em put her head around the door. "Fetch a cloth, would you!" Charles ordered. "Cindy's made one of her messes."

Exactly as if I were an untrained puppy, thought Lucinda, her cheeks burning. She picked up an empty platter and said to Fran, "We need more canapés."

But Leo broke in, "There's no time. I booked the table for seven-thirty."

"Before we go," Fran trilled, "I've got a little surprise for the girls. Y'all wait here now."

She slipped out to the hall closet and returned carrying three shopping bags that bore the name of an exclusive boutique.

"You spoil them, Fran," said Charles fondly.

"You girls can wear them tonight," Fran suggested. "It's supposed to rain later."

The bags contained identical vinyl raincoats—a silver one for Gina, gold for Trish and for Lucinda a bright cerise.

"Mom! How dreamy!" cried Trish, adjusting the huge shoulders to sit correctly.

Gina pirouetted in a swirl of silver. "Put yours on, Cindy," she said, her green eyes mocking. "Give us a fashion show."

Reluctantly Lucinda did. The fabric felt slippery under her fingers, and her face appeared as a round, white ball balanced on a glistening sailboard. The hem trailed on the ground in a bright pink puddle.

"It's a bit long," Del said dubiously.

"Cindy's a bit short," Gina countered. "A miniskirt would come to her ankles."

Lucinda thanked her stepmother, and then started to remove the enormous coat. "I think maybe I'll wait to have mine shortened before I wear it," she said.

"You're so tactless, Cindy," said Charles, his mouth set in a hard line.

"Now then, Cindy!" said Fran with an anxious look at her husband. "All you have to do is use the belt to hitch it up." She took a belt from the pocket and tied it tightly around Lucinda's little waist, pulling bunches of vinyl out over the top. "There! It's the right length now."

It might have been the right length, but that was all that was right about it. Trish and Gina looked like *Vogue* models in their garments; Lucinda felt like a two-tiered mushroom.

"I don't think it works," she said tentatively.

Her father cut in. "When your stepmother's taken the trouble to pick out an expensive gift, the least you could do is wear it. Don't be ungrateful."

Anxious to avoid an argument in front of Leo, Lucinda said quickly, "Of course I'll wear it. It's lovely."

"You don't appreciate how lucky you are," growled Charles.

"Now, Charlie, it's not her fault she can't wear stylish clothes," said Fran, in a misguided attempt to pour oil over troubled waters. "She lacks natural flair."

Leo, his voice sharp as a knife blade, snapped, "She certainly lacks *something*!"

There was an agonizing silence, and then Del cleared his throat. "We're going to be late, guys," he said, and everyone made a move for the door.

Lucinda felt as if she had been hit in the stomach. If she hadn't felt so shattered by Leo's bitter comment, she would have picked up some object, preferably something heavy, and hurled it at him. If this was his idea of "a cooling-off period" she didn't think much of it. Inwardly seething, she climbed into his car and looked resolutely out the window. *I hate him,* she thought, but she knew she didn't. Oh, at the moment she was so mad at him she could hardly breathe, but if she had really hated him that disparaging put-down would have been a scratch, not a wound that cut to the bone.

When they drew up in front of the restaurant it had started to rain. "So, Fran was right," remarked Leo, slamming the car door. "Well, it won't bother you. You're covered from head to foot in your new mac."

"Raincoat!" she snarled, tripping on the hem.

"Take the bloody thing off!" he growled, putting ungentle hands on her shoulders.

Furious, she attempted to hang on. "Let go! I'll catch cold."

"Better to catch pneumonia than split your skull on the pavement," he fumed, ripping the coat off her back.

"Sidewalk," she snarled, and swept ahead of him, past the goggling doorman.

She did not enjoy her dinner. She was in a rage with Leo, and as the meal progressed she became increasingly clumsy. Knives and forks jumped out of her hands, she spilled more salt than she could throw over her shoulder, and she kept dropping her napkin. After she'd managed to get the tablecloth caught in her bracelet and had spattered mint sauce all over herself, she sat glaring at her plate, wishing herself a million miles away.

Leo wasn't much of a host, either. His face had that dark brooding expression that made him look like a haughty eighteenth-century lord about to evict the tenants. Mercifully he declined Charles's invitation to have a nightcap at Cliff Top, and Lucinda determinedly took her place in the family car for the journey back.

"No point taking you out of your way," she told Leo frostily, although it wasn't out of his way at all.

He nodded curtly, and everyone exchanged goodnights outside the restaurant.

The next day was filthy. It was cold and wet, with a gusty wind that blew in Lucinda's face and misted her glasses—her old ones for this outing. *Yankee Doodle* was plunging about at her moorings like a bucking bronco intent on murder.

Leo drove up and Charles hailed him. "Going to be a great day!" Leo nodded and eyed Lucinda thoughtfully.

The three women got out of the station wagon, and while Lucinda started unpacking the food, Trish and Fran headed for *Yankee Doodle*, leaping aboard as easily as if the yacht were anchored in cement. While Lucinda was lugging the box of provisions, a loaf of bread fell to the ground. Swearing heartily, she kicked it.

"Mud sandwiches for lunch?" said a sardonic English voice.

"There's not going to be any lunch at this rate. Not that it matters. When the sea's this rough, Fran and Trish are too ill to think about food." She pushed the soggy bread back into the box. "They throw up like whales."

"I can't wait!" he said.

"Oh! You and Dad will be all right, lording around like admirals." She stared morosely at the heaving water. Out on the open sea it was going to be ghastly. Not only was it sure to be miserably uncomfortable, she would be scared. She was Maine born and bred: she respected the sea and its anger. It had claimed her maternal grandfather and great grandfather, and widowed Em as a young bride.

Without another word, Leo took the box from her. Lucinda returned to the car for the last remaining item, then struggled down the meadow after him. The wind felt strong enough to lean on, and it was getting worse.

When the box had been handed over, Leo leaped onto the heaving deck.

"Come on, Cindy," cried Trish. She smiled at Leo. "Getting Cindy aboard takes forever. She's about as surefooted as a hippo in a mudhole."

Just then Fran let out an eldritch screech. She was rummaging through the contents of the box, throwing aside apples and packages of nuts and raisins in her search. "My seasickness pills," she wailed, "they've been left behind."

"Are you sure?" asked Lucinda, hugging the chicken casserole she had made for their lunch to her breast.

"I remember putting them on the kitchen counter." Fran turned to her husband. "I left my pills at home, Charlie, and I'm feeling sick already!"

"Don't worry about it, hon," soothed Charles. "I've got some spare ones in my ditty bag." He squinted at his offspring. "Don't stand there gawking all morning, we want to cast off. And don't fall in, for Pete's sake, it's going to be a tough enough day without you adding to it." This was said with a tight smile, but it didn't hide his underlying contempt.

Lucinda looked at him. She looked at the tossing yacht. "I'm not coming," she said.

"Don't be ridiculous," growled Charles.

Trish put in, "It's not a gale-force wind."

"I don't care if it's a summer breeze, I'm not coming." She held up the casserole. "Here's lunch. All you have to do is heat it up."

"I can't go near the galley," her stepmother groaned. "The very thought of food makes me ill."

"Will you get on board this instant!" roared Charles. "It's inhuman, expecting Fran or Trish to get meals. You know what weak stomaches they've got."

"Fine!" said Lucinda. She flung the casserole as far out into the river as she could. It made a satisfying splash before sinking to the bottom like a stone.

She had the immense satisfaction of seeing her father at a loss for words, before turning on her heel and squelching back up the meadow.

She had nearly reached the gate, when she heard Leo call, "Lucinda, wait!" She saw him running after her.

"I won't change my mind," she said, when he reached her.

"I should hope not." He smiled at her. "I'll drive you home."

"No, thank you." She turned away. "I'll walk."

He caught her arm and pulled her close to him. "Don't be daft, darling." He brought his face down to hers and she saw that his eyes were brimming with love. "Darling, darling Lucinda," he said huskily, "will you please marry me?"

CHAPTER TEN

HE DIDN'T MEAN IT, of course. How could he? He despised her; he'd made that quite clear. A tide of anger swept over her, like the combers cresting the stormy Atlantic.

"Get away from me!" she cried with such passion that he let her go. "Just who do you think you are, Leo Grosvenor, playing your damn games? Friendly one moment—" her dark eyes flashed "—very friendly indeed if you had half a chance, and the next cold as ice."

"But darling—"

"Don't you 'darling' me, you English creep!"

"There was a reason—"

"I don't want to hear it," she spat at him. "I don't want to hear anything you have to say."

"But—"

"No! You listen to me. I've had it up to *here* with you—" furiously she slapped her chin "—and with dad, and Fran. The whole bunch of you—"

"Sweetheart, that's what I've been waiting for." He attempted to touch her but she hit at his hand.

"I don't give a hoot. All I want is for you to leave me alone. Go back to England . . . go to Africa for all

I care. But get out of my life, Leo. I never want to see you again." He took a step toward her. "I mean it."

"I do understand, darling."

"I don't care whether you do or not," she fumed, walking toward the road.

He called after her, "I'll phone you when you've had a chance to simmer down."

But she yelled back, "I'll hang up on you."

She struck out for home, buoyed up on a tide of burning rage. She heard him drive off, but he went in the opposite direction, and she didn't care. *I don't care!* The dam of years of pent-up humiliation had burst, and all she felt was a marvellous white-hot anger. The worm had turned with a vengeance.

When she was halfway home, the family drove up. They had decided to abandon their sailing, since two important crew members had abandoned ship. Strangely, Charles did not seem to be indignant. Indeed he seemed almost conciliatory when he offered to drive her the rest of the way.

"No thanks," she said crisply, not slowing her stride. "I'm enjoying the walk."

Fran leaned across her husband to ask, "What happened between you and Leo, Cindy? Did you have a fight?"

She went on walking, the station wagon crawling beside her. "He asked me to marry him."

"Cindy!" Fran cried. "How wonderful!"

"And I told him to get lost."

Fran's jaw dropped, and Charles said, bewildered, "But why, honey?"

She stopped then, and glared into the car. "Because he's an arrogant, conceited, overbearing *Brit*!" She shouted the last.

"But Cindy—" Trish began.

Lucinda stopped, "It's none of your business, Trish. Drop it!" And she stalked on.

Surprisingly, Trish did as she was told, and when Lucinda came down for dinner that evening, having spent the day in furious activity, baking bread and turning out cupboards, neither her stepsister nor the rest of the family referred to Leo. In fact, they treated Lucinda with muted solicitude, as if she had been ill and required special care.

Charles even went so far as to ask her if she would like to go sailing tomorrow, when the wind was supposed to have died down. "We could cruise the river," he suggested. "You like that."

But such consideration on his part was too late. It merely irritated Lucinda, and she curtly refused.

After dinner she sent Em up to her room to watch television, while she stayed in the kitchen cleaning every piece of silver she could lay her hands on. Fran came in after a while. She looked at Lucinda anxiously.

"Why don't you leave that, Cindy? Come and join your daddy and me. Maybe we could play a game of cards."

"No thanks," replied Lucinda, rubbing hard at a particularly tarnished fork.

"Well…would you fancy a cup of cocoa, honey?" She moved tentatively toward the stove.

"I've only just had dinner, Fran."

"Well..." She stood undecidedly in the doorway. "If you're sure there's nothing you want..."

"Not a thing." Lucinda found a cleaner spot on the piece of rag. "You'd better get back to Dad."

Fran hesitated, about to say more, then she thought better of it and quietly left the room.

Lucinda finished the silver and decided to join Em and watch television with her. On her way through the hall she remembered Leo's promise to call, so she went to the phone and removed the receiver from its cradle. Charles, who had come into the hall, watched her.

"You can put it back when I've gone to bed," she told him. "I don't want any phone calls tonight."

"Are you *sure*, Cindy?" asked her father.

She said firmly, "Quite sure," and went upstairs.

Her anger seemed to have purged her of dreams, and she slept well that night, waking to a calm day gilded with early fall sunshine.

After breakfast, during which her family furtively examined her as though searching for signs of mental illness, she went into the kitchen to tell Em that she'd decided to miss church this Sunday. She wouldn't have put it past Leo to be waiting for her there, and she didn't intend to put on a show for the churchgoers.

Fran had followed her, carrying some dirty dishes, an unusual gesture for Fran. "Cindy honey, why don't you come for a little drive," she said, tipping the plates in the sink. "We could have lunch at the club." She smiled with brittle gaiety. "A girls' day out. What do you say?"

Lucinda took the plates out of the sink and put them in the dishwasher. "Thanks, Fran, but I don't think so."

Fran frowned. "You have to relax sometime, honey."

"I'm perfectly relaxed," her stepdaughter replied tensely.

Fran looked dubious. "Well, if you're sure you're all right, honey...."

"I'm fine!" Lucinda snarled.

"Okay, don't get upset." She said to Em, "See that Miss Lucinda doesn't do too much today. She's under a strain."

"What strain?" inquired Em, when they were alone.

Lucinda pushed her fingers through her tumble of curls. "The strain of asserting myself at last, I think she means. That, and telling Leo I won't marry him."

"You won't? Why ever not?" Em began cautiously.

"Because he doesn't mean it," snapped Lucinda, her anger starting to smolder again. "Everything's a game with him. Everything's pretense. Pretending we slept together on that crummy island...pretending that we're having an affair—" Her voice wobbled dangerously. "I guess he was even pretending when he said he was my friend."

Em energetically screwed the lid back on a jar of jam. "That's the dumbest thing I ever heard, Lucinda. You don't need to be a genius to see that he's head over heels in love with you."

"Is that so?" Lucinda flared. "Then how come he's sweet as pie one minute, and cold as an Eskimo's nose the next? How do you explain that?"

"I don't know nothin' about Eskimos," said Em doggedly, "but I do know that the man's in love with you."

"Well, he's got a funny way of showing it."

"Maybe. But I'll bet my last dollar there's a reason. Did you try to find out what it was, before you sent him packin'?"

"Why should I?" railed Lucinda. "The man's been playing with me. Using me, and I'm not taking it anymore. Leo Grosvenor is nothing but a pig-headed...overbearing..."

"You love him," stated Em.

The kitchen clock ticked loudly. "That's beside the point," Lucinda said finally.

"I don't think it is." The girl opened her mouth to speak, but Em held up her hand. "Now you listen to me, Lucinda. Instead of screamin' your head off in my kitchen, go to Heron Cottage an' scream at him. Tell him all the things you've been tellin' me. It ain't fair, judgin' a person before he's had his say."

"He hasn't been fair to me," Lucinda muttered mulishly.

"Tell *him*," said Em, adding, "unless you're scared, of course."

"Of Leo? Don't be crazy!" She made a bound for the door. "I'll take his ears off."

She didn't bother with a coat, but snatching her purse from the hall table, dashed to her car and raced

out of the driveway at breakneck speed. The chain was
down at the entrance to the cottage lane, and several
loads of crushed stone had been laid on the rutted
surface to level it. She roared up it, scattering stones
behind her. A parking area had been cleared to one
side of the cottage, and she skidded to a stop beside
Leo's Buick. When she turned off the engine, the silence was filled with the sound of the sea and the
thudding of her heart.

She noticed that the balcony had been repaired and
the old paint had been stripped off. Then the front
door opened and Leo came out, and she stopped no-
ticing anything to do with renovations.

"I was just on my way to church to look for you,"
he said.

"I figured you might try that," she replied, "but I
want to see you alone, Leo Grosvenor, not in front of
the whole village."

He smiled and said, "That sounds hopeful."

"Don't count your chickens," she warned him.
"I've come for a showdown."

"Fair enough. Do you want to come inside? You
look cold."

The air was crisp and she was beginning to shiver,
so she nodded and followed him in.

Stepping into the hall was like stepping into a bowl
of light. The sea seemed to be reflected all around
them. It was like standing in the heart of a diamond.
"Oh," she cried, turning to him impulsively, "it's
lovely!"

"I'm glad you like it, Lucinda," he said. "It's important that you do."

Better not ask him why, she decided, and gave him an austere nod instead.

He opened the door to the living room. The walls had been painted a pale apricot. A beige whipcord sofa and matching armchair were standing on a cinnamon-colored rug. There was no other furniture in the room.

"This should warm us up," he said, putting a match to the fire that was laid in the hearth. A shower of sparks flew in a burst of orange gems.

"You've moved in, have you?" asked Lucinda. She thought wildly, I sound like a social worker on official business. I'll be asking him about the plumbing next.

"Let's say I'm camping here until I get your answer." He pulled her gently to sit down beside him on the sofa.

She snatched her hands away. "Stop playing games with me, Leo. It's not funny."

"Neither is what I feel for you," he said, and she sensed that he was in deadly earnest.

"Today is one of the days that you're nice to me, is it?" she asked bitterly.

"I plan to be more than nice to you if you'll let me." She didn't answer and he said softly, "I love you, Lucinda."

His eyes, which never left her face, were tender, but a flicker of her fast-dwindling anger made her say,

"That still doesn't explain the past couple of weeks." She glared. "Not to mention Friday night."

"The coat incident," he groaned. "God, Lucinda! Do you have any idea how it tears me apart seeing the way you let your family treat you? I get sick with anger, and when Fran threw that ridiculous coat at you, I hoped—oh, how I hoped!—that you'd thank her politely and throw it back. You're not blind, you must have seen how ludicrous you looked. But instead, the minute your father applied pressure, you meekly accepted, as usual, and I . . . I wanted to kill!"

"Me?"

He sighed ruefully. "Among others. I knew that until you rebelled, you'd never be free to be your own woman, make your own decisions."

"Why didn't you *tell* me all this, instead of being so . . . so cold?" she asked, a break in her voice.

He took her hands again, and this time she didn't pull them away. "I was angry, Lucinda. With you . . . with your family. I have a hot temper—"

She smiled. "You don't say!"

"And being remote is the only way I know to maintain some self-control. Besides, if I'd told you and you'd stood up to them, you'd have done it for me. It would have been just another example of Lucinda trying to please. You had to do it for yourself. You had to fight back because you refused to be treated like a second-class citizen any longer."

There was an imperious mew, and Boots stalked into the room and settled himself firmly in front of the fire. "Don't be selfish," said his master, moving him gently with the tip of his foot. "Let the lady have some warmth." Boots glared at him through his odd-colored eyes and vigorously licked where Leo's boot had touched him.

She gave a shaky laugh, for happiness had started to well up in her. "You're not going to say you loved me at first sight, are you?"

"Certainly not. During our famous weekend I disliked you intensely. But I was in a very bad mood, anyway. I was mad because I'd let myself be talked into going out in your father's blasted boat, and I took it out on you. Then, when I came back to Maine and saw you again...I didn't understand why I kept wanting to kiss you." The fire in his eyes flickered. "I should have known right away."

He cupped her pale face in his hands. "There is no one but you, Lucinda. There never will be. You're the beat of my heart. There's never been anyone like you in my life."

That was the truth. There had been plenty of women in his life, smart, sophisticated women. But not one of them had fired his blood the way this small scrap of a girl did. The fierceness of his desire for her had astonished him, until he realized that he was deeply, irrevocably, in love.

"And now my darling—" he stroked her hair with a hand that trembled a little "—will you marry me?"

On the wall the reflected glitter of sunlight seemed to dance with her joy, and she said very softly, "Yes, my Leo, I will."

"I'll teach you to love me," said proud, arrogant Leo with a catch in his voice. "You'll see."

"You don't have to teach me. I do already." She reached up to touch his hair and he caught her hand and kissed it; drawing her into his arms, kissing her cheeks, her hair, her lips. Desire washed over her like the tide.

"Let's get married soon," he said, his voice ragged, "before I go back to England."

She nodded happily, her cheek against his shoulder. Then she remembered Em and sat up. "I'll have to make some arrangements about Em. If I'm not in Small Port..."

He pulled her gently back against him. "How would the job of housekeeper for us suit her? She can baby-sit Boots when we're in England, and hire whoever she wants to do the heavy work."

She looked up at him, eyes shining. "You are a lovely man."

"And what about Cliff Top?" he asked. "Will you sell it to Charles?"

She thought a minute, then, "No," she said. "I'll let him live there for as long as he wants, but eventually I'd like our first son to inherit it."

His mouth curved up in that lovely smile of his. "Our first son will get Cloisters. Perhaps we should leave Cliff Top to our first daughter. And now, my darling—" reluctantly he got to his feet, pulling her with him "—now I think we should go and tell your father and Fran the news." He grinned. "And also make it plain that Fran will not be picking out your wedding dress."

On the veranda they stood for a minute, his arm around her shoulders, looking down at the ruffled hem of water curving around them. She asked, "If I'd said no, what would you have done with this place?"

"Left it forever," he replied somberly.

She knew that he meant it. Heron Cottage would have been shuttered and deserted again...and so would her heart.

"But you always get what you want," she reminded him softly.

He hugged her tighter and said, "If you'd said no, I would have died inside. It's as simple as that."

He started down the path, but Lucinda hesitated. "What is it, darling?" he asked.

"Nothing." She took his outstretched hand and went with him to the car, but for a moment she had distinctly heard the sound of two little ghosts laughing.

HARLEQUIN
Romance®

Coming Next Month

#3043 MOUNTAIN LOVESONG Katherine Arthur
Lauren desperately needs help at her northern California holiday lodge, so
when John Smith, handyman *extraordinaire*, appears out of nowhere, he
seems the answer to her prayers. The only question—how long can she depend
on him?

#3044 SWEET ILLUSION Angela Carson
Dr. Luke Challoner, arrogant and domineering, expects everyone to bow to his
will. He is also one of the most attractive men Marion has ever met—which
doesn't stop her from standing up for herself against him!

#3045 HEART OF THE SUN Bethany Campbell
Kimberly came home to Eureka Springs to nurse a broken heart. Alec
Shaughnessy came to examine Ozark myth and folklore. Both become
entangled in a web of mystery that threatens to confirm an old prophesy—that
the women in Kimberly's family might never love happily.

#3046 THAT CERTAIN YEARNING Claudia Jameson
Diane's heart goes out to vulnerable young Kirsty, but warning bells sound
when she meets Kirsty's dynamic and outspoken uncle, Nik Channing. Yet she
has to support Kirsty, even if it means facing up to her feelings . . . and to Nik.

#3047 FULLY INVOLVED Rebecca Winters
Fight fire with fire—that was how Gina Lindsay planned to win back her ex-
husband. Captain Grady Simpson's career as a firefighter had destroyed his
marriage to Gina three years earlier. But now she's returned to Salt Lake
City—a firefighter, too. . . .

#3048 A SONG IN THE WILDERNESS Lee Stafford
Amber is horrified when noted journalist Lucas Tremayne becomes writer-
in-residence at the university where she is secretary to the dean. For Luke
had played an overwhelming part in her teenage past—one that Amber prefers
stay hidden. . . .

Available in April wherever paperback books are sold, or through
Harlequin Reader Service:

In the U.S.
901 Fuhrmann Blvd.
P.O. Box 1397
Buffalo, N.Y. 14240-1397

In Canada
P.O. Box 603
Fort Erie, Ontario
L2A 5X3

You'll flip . . . your pages won't!
Read paperbacks *hands-free* with

Book Mate • I

The perfect "mate" for all your romance paperbacks

Traveling • Vacationing • At Work • In Bed • Studying • Cooking • Eating

Perfect size for all standard paperbacks, this wonderful invention makes reading a pure pleasure! Ingenious design holds paperback books OPEN and FLAT so even wind can't ruffle pages — leaves your hands free to do other things. Reinforced, wipe-clean vinyl-covered holder flexes to let you turn pages without undoing the strap . . . supports paperbacks so well, they have the strength of hardcovers!

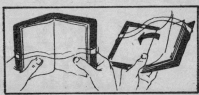

Pages turn WITHOUT opening the strap

SEE-THROUGH STRAP

Reinforced back stays flat

Built in bookmark

BOOK MARK

BACK COVER HOLDING STRIP

10 x 7¼ opened
Snaps closed for easy carrying, too

This April, don't miss Harlequin's new Award of
Excellence title from

elusive as the unicorn

*When Eve Eden discovered that Adam
Gardener, successful art entrepreneur, was
searching for the legendary English artist, The
Unicorn, she nervously shied away. The Unicorn's
true identity hit too close to home....*

*Besides, Eve was rattled by Adam's
mesmerizing presence, especially in the light
of the ridiculous coincidence of their names—
and his determination to take advantage of it!
But Eve was already engaged to marry her
longtime friend, Paul.*

*Yet Eve found herself troubled by the different
choices Adam and Paul presented. If only the
answer to her dilemma didn't keep eluding her...*

HP1258-i